A Share of Freedom

June Rae Wood
AR B.L.: 4.8
Points: 8.0   UG

A Share of
Freedom

June Rae Wood

Hyperion Paperbacks for Children
New York

$\mathscr{W}$ith love to Woody, my husband and best friend, and to Sami, the light of my life.

$\mathscr{W}$ith special thanks for M. R., who tried to "fix" everything, and to P. H., who shared her pain.

First Hyperion Paperback edition 1996

Text © 1994 by June Rae Wood.

First published in hardcover in 1994. Reprinted by permission of G. P. Putnam's Sons, a division of the Putnam & Grosset Group.

Printed in the United States of America.
3 5 7 9 10 8 6 4

Library of Congress Cataloging-in-Publication Data

Wood, June Rae.
A share of Freedom / June Rae Wood.
p.   cm.
Summary: Thirteen-year-old Freedom who, along with her stepbrother, is being raised by an embittered alcoholic mother, longs to know who her father is and why his identity has always been a secret.
ISBN 0-7868-1085-8 (pbk.)
[1. Family problems—Fiction. 2. Alcoholism—Fiction.
3. Brothers and sisters—Fiction. 4. Unmarried mothers—Fiction.
5. Fathers and daughters—Fiction.] I. Title.
PZ7.W84965Sh   1996
[Fic]—dc20

95-40522

CONTENTS

1

THE TROPHY

"Ninety-four degrees. It's too blamed hot to be traipsing all over town," grumbled Mama, shading her eyes as she peered ahead at the digital sign at the bank.

I wrinkled my nose at the alcohol on her breath. The little nip she'd taken to get her up and going smelled like a brewery in the heat. The sign was flashing the message, "Have a safe and happy Fourth of July," and I frowned. How could we enjoy family day at the fairgrounds if Mama didn't lighten up?

"Today's a scorcher, and we're headed for the hottest place on the planet," she muttered. "I don't know how I let you kids talk me into this."

"Because it's a holiday and Freedom's birthday," said Jackie, my eight-year-old brother. He was hanging on to one side of Mama, while I was penning her in on the other.

"I know it's your sister's birthday," she said. "I was there when it happened."

I glanced at my mother, who was half a head shorter than I. It was a mystery how someone as small

and delicate as she could have given birth to someone
like me, Freedom Jo Avery. I was tall and gawky and
freckled, and if the hump on my nose had been on my
back, I could have passed for a camel.

Mama was pretty—or would have been if she'd
taken better care of herself. She was thin, with a
potbelly that barely showed under the big square
pockets of her checkered sundress. Her hair, honey-
colored and wavy, looked slightly greasy in the sun,
and the comb had left tracks above her ears. Automatically, I touched my own dishwater-blond hair that
brushed my shoulders, glad I'd washed it this morning
and let it hang loose.

"If the clutch hadn't gone out on that blamed old
truck, we wouldn't have to walk every time we took
a notion to go someplace," said Mama.

Now that we had her this far, I hoped she wasn't
going to turn around and head back home, although
it wouldn't have surprised me if she did. I never knew
what to expect from her. After keeping Jackie and me
guessing all week, this morning she had finally agreed
to go to the fairgrounds, because she was too broke to
buy me a birthday present.

Mama was forever complaining that we never had
two nickels left to rub together after rent and groceri-
ies, yet somehow there was always enough to buy her
a bottle. Ever since my stepfather had run off with
another woman, drinking seemed to be the only thing
she cared about.

"Slow down, Freedom," she said as she mopped
sweat from her forehead. "When I agreed to do this,

I didn't plan on running all the way to the fair-grounds."

We weren't running. We weren't even walking very fast. But I slowed my steps to a crawl and resigned myself to missing the opening ceremony that would be starting at one o'clock in the grandstand. I'd learned by now not to rile Mama, because it gave her an excuse to drink.

Besides, she was right about the day being a scorcher. A hot breeze was blowing in my face, and the sidewalk was burning my feet right through the soles of my tennis shoes. Still, I wasn't going to let the heat ruin my double celebration—the Fourth of July and my thirteenth birthday. It was the one day in the year when I felt comfortable with my patriotic name.

Mama didn't have much imagination, so I never could figure out how she'd dreamed up such a name as Freedom. Kids who heard it for the first time usually snickered and looked me up and down as if expecting me to be draped in an American flag.

I wasn't wearing a flag, but a pair of cutoff blue jeans and the Gabriel Gremlins T-shirt I'd bought at the secondhand store. The shirt was a bargain at fifty cents and only a little faded, and the tiny, scorpion-shaped ink spot on the left shoulder was barely notice-able. We moved to Gabriel six months ago from Kansas City, and I'd hoped to become a part of the crowd. That idea had fizzled out like a dud fire-cracker, but the shirt almost made me feel as if I belonged.

Although Gabriel, Missouri, was Mama's hometown, it hadn't shown me much so far. If it hadn't been for Alice, my one and only friend, seventh grade here would have been a total washout.

"Freedom, answer me," said Mama.

"What?"

"You're lost in that dream world again. Half the time when I talk to you, I don't know if you're hearing me or not."

"I'm listening."

"Are you sure it's not going to cost us to get in? I'd hate to find out we walked all this way for nothing."

"I'm sure, Mama. The posters said everything's free but the refreshments."

"What kind of refreshments?" asked Jackie as the breeze riffled his white-blond hair, making it stand up like dandelion fluff.

"Slushees, cotton candy, corn dogs," I said. "The kinds of things they have at a county fair."

"I want a cherry Slushee. One so cold it hurts my teeth."

"Don't be begging me for a lot of junk food," cautioned Mama. "I've got just four dollars to last till the end of the week."

I patted my pocket. "I've got money."

"You won't have if you blow it on junk. I hate to see you wasting your baby-sitting money on something that'll be gone in five minutes."

I had to bite my tongue to keep from saying, "At least Slushees won't give us a hangover." I couldn't explain it, but every time Mama said anything to me lately, a hateful comeback popped into my head.

"I hear the band playing *The Star-Spangled Banner*," said Jackie. His eyes sparkled, and I could tell he was itching to run ahead and see what was happening. He held himself back, though, and kept plodding along with us.

At the entrance to the fairgrounds, I picked up a schedule that listed contests and demonstrations all afternoon, a band concert in the evening, and a fireworks display after dark. The event I most looked forward to was the old-fashioned spelling bee. It was the one contest I thought maybe I could win, because it depended on smarts, rather than popularity, coordination, or luck.

"What'll we do first?" asked Jackie as the crowd hustled us along into the fairgrounds.

"The spelling bee," I replied. "It starts in just a few minutes at the grandstand."

"Aw, Freed," he said, his face darkening.

I knew that to a little boy who didn't read very well, the spelling bee would be the most boring thing on earth. "Bear with me, Cotton Top. Then I'll watch you in the relay races the rest of the afternoon."

"OK," he said, hunching his shoulders and hiking up his shorts. "Let's get it over with."

"Don't be such a killjoy," said Mama. "Your sister's gonna go out there and whip everybody in town. She's got what it takes to be somebody someday."

"Please, Mama, not so loud," I said. The crowd was making Mama nervous, and it showed in her voice.

"Don't you be telling me what to do, Freedom Avery."

"I'm sorry. It's just—well, I might not win. The competition'll be really tough."

Mama wouldn't leave it alone. "Don't be so modest. You could whip old Noah Webster himself. You showed that bunch at school just how smart you are, didn't you?"

"She's smart enough to know where to buy cookies," piped a voice behind me, and I whirled around and saw Laura Nell Gentry and Melissa Baumgardner from my class.

A pain stabbed my stomach. That happened when I was nervous or worried about something or within spitting distance of Laura Nell. "Grow up!" I snapped, glaring at her.

The girls giggled and ran away laughing.

I turned back around and forced myself to keep walking as great rivers of sweat raced down between my shoulder blades.

"What was that all about?" asked Mama.

"Nothing," I mumbled, knowing it was no use trying to explain. Mama wouldn't remember the cookie incident, because she'd been drunk when it happened.

I could see it, plain as day. Mama nursing a bottle of cheap whiskey. Laura Nell dropping by the house with another girl, selling Girl Scout cookies. Mama ordering ten boxes. Ten boxes, when we couldn't afford even one! I'd snatched away the order blank and torn it to bits, saying, "Go away! If we want cookies, we'll go to the grocery store!"

Laura Nell wasn't even a Girl Scout, but now "cookies" was her buzz word, and she knew it was good for getting a rise out of me.

Mama was staring in the direction of Laura Nell and Melissa. "There has to be a reason those girls were acting like half-wits."

"Some people don't need a reason, Mama," I said. "Just drop it." But I couldn't stop thinking about it myself.

We headed for the grandstand, where people were gathering for the spelling bee. My pain eased a bit when I spied Alice standing under a "No Alcoholic Beverages" sign. She was blinking like a toad in a hailstorm as she peered into the crowd, and I figured her new contact lenses were still giving her fits.

She had her little sister by the hand, and I smiled to myself as I thought how the genes in that family must run toward string bean. Alice was even taller and gawkier than I, and Tina, the same age as Jackie, was a scaled-down version of Alice. Their mother made all their clothes, and today they were dressed identically in white shirts and yellow shorts with suspenders. They reminded me of two half-peeled bananas.

Alice's gaze landed on me, and she started waving.

"That's Alice," I said to Mama as I waved back. I had never invited Alice over, and I told myself it was because our house was just too small and shabby. Deep down, I knew it was because Mama drank.

When we reached the girls, I said, "I didn't expect to see you today."

"The relatives aren't coming until suppertime, so

we decided to hang out with you guys for a while. I knew I'd catch you here," said Alice, glancing curiously at my mother.

"This is our mom," I said. "Mama, meet Alice and Tina."

"Come on," said Tina. "Let's get a seat at the top of the bleachers." She grabbed Jackie's hand, and off they went.

Alice rolled her watery eyes at her sister's rudeness and looked at Mama. "Hi, Mrs. Ramsdale. I guess you came to watch Freedom beat the socks off everybody in the spelling bee."

Mama smiled. "She can do it. She's got a memory that won't quit."

It was true. Once I'd seen a word in print, I could remember ever afterwards how it was spelled. But I felt self-conscious about Mama's bragging, especially since Alice was a superduper writer but couldn't spell worth a hoot.

"I know," said Alice as she pushed back a strand of her kinky permed hair. "Just when I think I've written a story that's perfect, she reads it and finds a plethora of misspelled words."

I grinned at her use of "plethora," a noun that found its way into all of her stories and most of her conversations.

"Then you're not entering the spelling bee?" asked Mama.

"Heavens, no. I'll leave that to the walking dictionary." Alice batted her eyes and wiped moisture from their corners with her fingers.

"How are the contacts?" I ventured. "Still giving you trouble?"

"Bummer. Same as wearing toenails in my eyes."

Mama chuckled, and I knew she'd taken a liking to Alice.

"I'll leave you two to get acquainted," I said. "I've got to go sign up."

"We'll be rooting for you," called Alice as I headed for the registration table.

While awaiting my turn at the table, I glanced around at the competition. The contest was for people twelve and up, and there was about an even mix of kids and grownups.

Laura Nell and Melissa were signing up, and when they saw me, they started giggling. Let them giggle. They couldn't do a school assignment without putting their heads together, as if they had only one good brain between them. I wondered which one would use it today.

I recognized two teachers, the mayor, and a candidate for sheriff. One lady, a secretary maybe, was wearing a watermelon-colored pullover that said, "My boss went to the Bahamas, and all I got was this dumb T-shirt."

When I saw Lydia Barton in line behind me, I turned away so she wouldn't notice me, and studied her out of the corner of my eye. She had on the new style Gremlins T-shirt, the kind with the hot pink logo, and her short dark hair was feathered away from her face. I envied her cute pug nose and tanned, smooth skin that never had a freckle or a zit.

I hadn't seen Lydia since the end of school, when I'd stolen her thunder at the awards ceremony. Until I came along, she'd been named top student every year, which in this little burg was supposed to be a status symbol or something. Even though I'd worked my way to the top spot, the status hadn't rubbed off on me. There'd been a question about whether I would qualify for the honor because I was a transfer student, but when Mama mentioned lawsuit to the principal, he decided that my Kansas City grades would count.

Anyway, now I had two good reasons for feeling uncomfortable around Lydia. First, she'd lost out by only a fraction of a percentage point, which would make anybody mad. And second, she was rich. I had it from Alice's own mouth that Lydia's folks kept two cases of Pepsi on hand at all times. A plethora of Pepsi. Absolute proof that she lived in the lap of luxury.

At the registration table, I filled out my card and handed it to the lady in charge.

"Freedom Jo Avery," she said. "What a great name for the Fourth of July." She smiled and pinned a big number "22" on my shirt.

I smiled back and walked up to the stage, past Laura Nell and Melissa. I could feel them talking about me, but I took my place in line and stared out toward the audience. Mama and Alice were searching for Tina and Jackie high up in the bleachers, where batches of kids were sprawled out in the sun like wilted posies. The older crowd was sitting in the shaded lower seats. I drew a few deep breaths, psyching myself up for the spelling bee.

There were twenty-six contestants, and when the last one was on stage, the emcee went to the microphone. He welcomed everyone and read the rules:

"After the pronouncer gives a word, the contestant will step to the microphone, repeat the word, then spell it. If he spells it correctly, he goes to the end of the line to compete again. If not, he's out of the running. This process will continue until there are only two people left. If one of them misspells a word, the other must spell it correctly to be declared the winner. At no time will prompting from the audience be allowed."

When the emcee turned the microphone over to the pronouncer, Rufus Finley, I felt myself relax. "Mr. Friendly," as Alice and I called him, was one of my favorite people, and someday I hoped to be as good a librarian as he was. In the spirit of the Fourth, he was wearing red Bermuda shorts and an American flag T-shirt. His round bald head was hidden beneath a Royals baseball cap.

Mr. Finley started us off easy. He sailed through the line the first time and lost only one contestant, who misspelled "recognize."

The second time through, the words were a bit harder, and six people went down. Laura Nell lost out on "bated," Melissa on "receipt," and one of the teachers on "consensus."

In the next round, we went from nineteen contestants down to ten as the words got trickier. The mayor misspelled "niche." I got "moccasin" right.

Eventually, it came down to three of us—Lydia, the secretary, and me—and the ache in my stomach let me know it was still there. When I stepped to the microphone, Mama yelled from the bleachers, "Go get 'em, Freedom," and I felt heat rush to my face. Please, Mama, I begged silently, don't embarrass me now.

Mr. Finley grinned at me and pronounced the word, "witticize."

"Witticize," I repeated calmly, but my mind was racing. What in thunder kind of word was that? I cleared my throat and said, "W-I-T-T-I-C-I-Z-E."

"That's absolutely correct, young lady," said Mr. Finley, so I went back to the end of the line.

Lydia stepped up next, and Mr. Finley asked her to spell "maneuver."

"M-A-N-E-U-V-E-R."

"You've spelled the word correctly, but you didn't pronounce it first. I'm sorry."

Lydia groaned and walked off the stage.

I tried to draw a deep breath, but it made my stomach hurt worse and I cut it short. Glancing sideways at the secretary, I saw her eyeing me.

"Looks like it's just you and me, kid," she whispered. "Where'd you learn to spell so well?"

"I read all the time," I whispered back. In the lunch line, in the bathroom, even washing dishes with my book propped up on the sink.

She flashed me a thumbs-up and made her way to the mike.

"Ennui," said Mr. Finley.

The secretary jerked her head back and said, "What?"

My heart lurched. Was it possible she didn't know how to spell "ennui"? The word meant extreme boredom, and Alice used it a lot. I could almost hear her saying, "If Reba Sullivan tells me about the squirrels in her attic one more time, I'm going to die of ennui."

"Ennui," repeated Mr. Finley.

"Ennui," said the secretary. She cleared her throat and spelled the word like it sounds: "O-N-W-E-E."

"I'm sorry, that's not correct. But you're not disqualified until the other contestant spells it correctly. Freedom?" From the look on Mr. Finley's face, he didn't expect me to have even heard the word before.

I gave him my best smile and stepped up to the mike. "Ennui. E-N-N-U-I."

"Hot dog! We have a winner!" cried Mr. Finley, slapping me on the back. "Ladies and gentlemen, this is Freedom Jo Avery, spelling whiz."

The crowd started clapping and cheering, and the secretary grabbed my hand and shook it. When Mr. Finley presented me with a trophy, a man jumped up on stage and took my picture.

"Freedom. That's quite a name," the photographer said as he removed a notebook from his pocket. "I need your age, your address, and your parents' names."

"Why?"

"Because your picture's going to be in this evening's *Gabriel Gazette*. The editor's saving a hole for the winner on the front page. Hurry now. We go to press in an hour."

"Today's my birthday. I'm thirteen. I live at two-twenty-seven Dogwood Lane, Apartment B, and my mother's name is Mary Margaret Ramsdale."

He wrote that down and waited for more.

"Just put my mother's name. That's all," I mumbled. How could I tell a total stranger that I didn't know who or where my father was?

The photographer closed his notebook. "The editor's never gonna believe that somebody named Freedom won on the Fourth of July. Congratulations," he said and hurried down the steps.

"I'm proud of you," said Mr. Finley. "You deserve that trophy."

I looked at the tall, gleaming object in my hand—a robed woman with a lamp of learning. Below her was the inscription, "Spelling Champion, Fourth of July. Knowledge Is Freedom."

"Take it to Dobson's Jewelry Store next week, and they'll engrave your name on it for free."

"Thanks, Mr. Friendly, I will. Thanks a lot."

I jumped down from the stage, and Lydia came up to me, saying, "Well, Freedom Avery, you beat me again. Congratulations, I think."

Was this a joke? I narrowed my eyes and glanced behind her, to see if her friends were watching, but there was only a row of old ladies smiling at me. "Thanks," I mumbled. "You didn't do so bad yourself. It was the rule that stopped you."

"Whatever. I was nervous, but you stayed cool as could be."

I'd faked her out then, but I was burning up now. Lydia was looking at my left shoulder, and I had a horrible thought. Did she recognize my T-shirt? What if it was one of her rejects? I felt the ink-blot scorpion crawling on me, stinging right down to the bone.

"Well, enjoy your summer. I plan to give you a run for your money in eighth grade," said Lydia with a laugh, and she sailed away.

Knees quivering, armpits wet, I waited for Alice and Mama and the kids, who were in the flow of traffic coming down the steps. When I caught Alice's eye, I held up the trophy in shaky triumph.

"That's nice, Freedom," said someone sweetly beside me, "but it's not as good as cookies."

If I'd been blind in both eyes, I'd have known it was Laura Nell Gentry.

2

BIG-SHOT WHIZ KID

"Three cheers for Freedom!" yelled Alice, giving the "V" for victory sign.

Mama reached toward me, and I thought I might get a hug. Instead, she grabbed the trophy and held it to her chest. "I guess you showed them," was all she said. No hug, no pat on the back. I was disappointed, but not surprised. Mama wasn't much for hugging.

Jackie caught my hand and squeezed it. "Good job, Freed. Now can Tina and I try to win something, too?"

"Sure thing, Cotton Top." I pulled my schedule from my pocket and started reading the events to him. "First comes the splash dash, then tug-of-war—"

"Where's the splash dash?" interrupted Tina.

"Over by the cattle barn."

"Well, come on then. Let's go," she said, and darted away towing Jackie.

Mama and Alice and I followed at a civilized pace.

"Are you going to enter anything?" Alice asked me.

"Nope. Clumsy as I am, I'd trip over my own feet."

"Same here," she replied. "When I want the world

to know I'm gonky, I'll just go to the newspaper office and take out a classified ad."

That was another thing about Alice. She made up words like "gonky," which wasn't in the dictionary but described her and me to a T.

At the splash dash, kids were putting on plastic helmets with paper cups taped to the top, then lining up by a washtub to have the cups filled with water.

After helping Jackie and Tina get set up, Alice and I joined Mama, who was sitting on the grass, polishing my trophy on her dress tail.

When the race began, the kids shot away from the starting line, stiff as little toy soldiers. It was comical, watching them speed up, slosh water, slow down, then speed up again.

Tina crossed the line first, but the kid behind her won because he still had half a cup of water, while hers was almost empty. Tina came running over to us, complaining that the boy had cheated. Jackie just swiped the water off his face and said, "That was fun! What's next?"

All afternoon, the kids kept us flitting about like butterflies, going from one contest to another. We bought Slushees and sat to watch a dance demonstration, but Jackie and Tina gulped down their drinks and were off and running before the dance was over.

"I wish I had their energy," sighed Mama. "I'd bottle it up and sell it and make a million dollars." She slurped at her Slushee and hiccuped, and that made all three of us laugh.

While the spider race was being organized, Alice

and I went to the restroom. We were washing our hands when she caught my eye in the mirror. "Your mom's nice—not at all like I expected." Her face flushed, and she said, "I'm sorry. That didn't come out right."

"It's my own fault. I talk too much. Mama's OK, until she's had too much to drink."

"I know what you mean. My Uncle Lee's a nice guy until he gets a few beers under his belt. Then he thinks he's a lady's man or something." Alice shuddered and added, "Yuk. I don't know how anybody can stand beer. Far as I'm concerned, they can pour that stuff right back into the horse."

Giggling, we left the restroom and collided with Henry Bockelman, who was coming out of the men's room. The force of our impact on his soft belly sent his combination toothpick and ear spoon flying. It was a "treasure" he'd found in a box of junk at his secondhand store. He claimed it was solid gold, but it plunked on the sidewalk like a plugged nickel.

"Hey! Watch where— Oh, it's you, Freedom. What's the big hurry?"

"Sorry, Henry, we weren't paying attention," I said as I retrieved the shiny gadget and handed it to him.

He wiped the pointed end on his pants and stuck it back in his mouth. The cupped end was for digging wax from his ears. "I'd go broke if I didn't pay any closer attention to business than that."

"You'll never go broke," I said, "as long as you've got that solid gold doodad."

That seemed to please him. "That's a fact, girl, that's a fact. You two have fun and don't run over any more helpless old men," he said as he shuffled away.

Henry was about as helpless as a den of rattle-snakes. He considered himself a wheeler-dealer, but since I'd wised up to his ways, I could dicker for a bargain until he was blue in the face.

Alice looked back at Henry as we started up the sidewalk. "Who *is* that guy?" she asked.

"Henry Bockelman from Second Time Around."

"Oh. The glorified dump."

"You always turn your nose up at the junk store, and you've never even been inside it. Henry's got a lot of good stuff. Where else could you buy a pair of Nikes for two dollars?" I almost stuck out one foot to show her, but I caught myself in time. The shoes might have once been Lydia's, too.

"OK, OK. Sorry if I stepped on your toes. Who am I to talk?" Alice linked her arm with mine and teased, "Step right up, folks. We're Alice Murdock and Freedom Avery. We wear homemades and hand-me-downs. Come one, come all, and see the grab bag friends."

I chuckled. Alice was terrific. It wouldn't make any difference to her if my whole wardrobe came from Lydia's closet.

We circled around the crowd and sat beside Mama on a bench to watch the spider race. Each "spider" was made up of two kids hustling along on all fours, one on top of the other. Jackie and Tina were part-ners, and they couldn't synchronize their movements. The effect was of a huge, clumsy creature that had absolutely no control of its body.

By the time the race was over, Mama was limp with

laughter. I was laughing, too, not so much at Jackie and Tina, but because the holiday seemed to be working magic. Mama was having fun. She hadn't carried on like that since before my stepfather, Leonard, left home. It was the perfect birthday present.

We watched a free-style bike riding demonstration and the three-legged race. Finally, Alice glanced at her watch and said, "Bad as I hate to leave a good party, we've got to go home for the barbecue."

"But I haven't won a prize yet," argued Tina. Her lower lip was pooched out so far, I thought she'd step on it.

"Neither has Jackie, but you don't hear him complaining," said Alice.

Tina stomped her foot. "They've got more contests and the band concert and the fireworks. I'm not leaving."

"Oh, yes, you are," said Alice, "or I'll be forced to tell Dad who dropped his electric razor in the toilet."

"You wouldn't do that."

"Try me," said Alice.

Tina kicked her sister in the shin. "I don't like you. You're mean and hateful and ugly with that kinky hairdo."

I glanced at Mama. If Jackie or I acted like that, she would slap us silly. I hadn't noticed before, but her eyes were glassy, and her face was red.

"So maybe I'll shave it off, like you did your Barbie doll," said Alice, grabbing hold of Tina's suspenders where they crisscrossed in the back. She turned to us and said, "I'm glad you won the trophy, Freedom. It was nice meeting you, Mrs. Ramsdale. See you later."

She pointed Tina toward the main gate and tried to steer her from behind. When that didn't work, she stepped in front and started pulling, while Tina yelled and dragged her feet.

We watched the struggle until the girls were out of sight.

"Someone should take a switch to that kid," muttered Mama.

That seemed to be the turning point. From then on, we didn't have much fun, and I was relieved when the last contest—the turtle race—rolled around.

I went with Jackie to help him pick out a turtle. He snatched up the first one that stuck its head out of its shell. "I'm calling him Speedway, for good luck."

I gave him an "OK" sign and went over to stand with Mama.

Since the race depended on the moods of the turtles more than anything else, we had a long wait. As the turtles began poking their heads out and taking a few cautious steps within the circle, I studied the men who were coaching their kids from the sidelines, and wondered if any of them were like the dad I'd never known.

After my stepfather left home, I was old enough and curious enough to start asking questions about my real father. Mama would either yell at me or clam up, depending on how much she'd had to drink, but she wouldn't give me any information I could use. My father was a part of her life she wanted to forget. I guess she didn't know her secrecy had left me with a hole in my soul.

I'd started ranking other kids' fathers on a scale of

one to ten, with one being the worst and ten being the All-American Dad I was dreaming up for myself. Now, during the turtle race, I had all shapes and sizes of men to scrutinize. That fellow in the red tank top and shorts was homely as mud, but he was yelling encouragement to his child. I gave him an eight. The guy next to him was loud and insulting. I gave him a two. A curly-headed man with a baby in his backpack was calling softly, "Don't spook him, Sandy. He's moving right along." Nine and a half.

". . . dream world again," said Mama, nudging me with my trophy.

"I'm sorry. What?"

"I said stop popping your knuckles. It's not lady-like. Come on. I've got to get out of this sun before it cooks my brain."

I followed her as she headed for the shade of the home economics building and plopped down on the grass.

We'd been sitting only a couple of minutes when I smelled the sickly sweet odor of whiskey. I jerked my head around and saw Mama slipping a medicine bottle into her dress pocket. Popping my knuckles wasn't *ladylike,* but my mother had been swigging from a bottle like some derelict. "Mama," I croaked, "what are you doing?"

I saw the glint in her eyes that meant back off, but I didn't heed the warning. "Couldn't you have left that stuff at home for one day?"

"Don't lecture me, Freedom," she snapped in a voice that caused several people to turn around and stare at us. "You're the one who wanted to drag me out here today, knowing I can't stand the crowds and the heat. I'm just having a little nip."

I was horrified. How many little nips had she had, anyway? How many people had seen her sneaking the bottle from her pocket? I glanced around nervously, expecting to see Hilda Harbaugh from the Child Protection Agency swooping down on us.

Miss Harbaugh was a social worker. She'd been to our house three times since we'd moved to Gabriel, acting on tips from some busybody that Jackie and I were being neglected and abused. On the last visit, she'd told Mama to control her drinking, or there was a chance she could lose us to a foster home. Mama had promised to stay dry, which she hadn't, although she had slacked off some. And here she was now, making a public spectacle of herself. "But Mama," I said, "think about Miss Harbaugh—"

"Don't 'but Mama' me. I don't want to hear it. Nag, nag, nag. That's all you do." Her voice grew louder as she shook a finger at me and said, "I'm thirty-two years old and perfectly capable of making decisions all by myself. I don't need a nosy old social worker or a big-shot whiz kid to keep me in line."

"What's the problem, ladies?" someone asked, and I looked up into the stern face of a security guard.

"No problem, officer," said Mama. She got up, brushing off her backside. "My daughter and I are just having a friendly disagreement." She leaned very close to him and whispered, "She turned thirteen today, and you know what they say about teenagers."

"Madam," said the guard as he backed away from her breath, "have you been drinking?"

Easing the bottle from her pocket so that its neck showed, she winked at the man. "It's just a little antacid, for when she gives me heartburn."

"I'm going to have to ask you to leave," said the guard. "This is city property, and alcoholic beverages are not allowed."

I buried my face in my hands. The gesture reminded me of Jackie, hiding his eyes when he was little. He'd thought if he couldn't see us, we couldn't see him. It didn't work. I could feel a million eyes staring at me.

"We can't leave," argued Mama. "My kids'll miss out on the fun."

"Your kids can stay, but I'm afraid you'll have to go, because you're under the influence of alcohol."

"Now, look here, officer—"

Mama was throwing our future to the wind, all for the sake of a bottle of whiskey. I had a vision of her being arrested and Jackie and me being hauled off to a foster home. Pain seared my stomach like a red-hot poker as I pushed myself to my feet. "We were just going," I said, reaching for my mother's arm. "Come on, Mama, Jackie's had enough excitement for one day. We don't want him to overdo it and get sick."

She blinked at me and started to resist, while I prayed that God wouldn't let her make a bigger scene. I felt my life hanging in the balance, so I added, "You can drink all you want to at home."

That did the trick. Mama edged up close to the

guard and said, "We've got to go home now. My little boy doesn't know when to quit."

And neither do you, Mama, I wanted to shout. Blindly, I picked up my trophy and steered her away. I searched for Jackie, but all the faces in the crowd, so ordinary just minutes ago, had become a sea of leering eyeballs.

Finally, Jackie came dancing around in front of us, showing off his turtle and a little plastic race car. "Freedom, did you see Speedway win? Now I've got a prize, too."

"That's nice," I said, "but we've got to go home."

"Go home? But—"

"Don't argue."

"But it's not over yet. What about the band concert and the fireworks?"

"We'll miss the concert. We can see the fireworks from home."

His jaw jutted out, and he planted his feet stubbornly in the dirt. "Go on without me. I'm staying here."

He was using Tina's tactics. I looked to Mama to do something, but she was taking another nip and was no help at all. A quick glance at the crowd told me we were still the main attraction at the fairgrounds. "Jackie, we've got to go home. *Now!*"

"No."

Shaking my trophy at him, I muttered, "Jackie Ramsdale, if you don't turn around right this minute and aim for the gate, I'm going to conk you over the head and drag you out of here."

I wouldn't have done it, but I made a believer out of him. He obeyed, kicking at the ground with every step and mumbling that he didn't have to do anything some dumb old girl told him to do.

As we left through the main gate, I heard the band strike up *Yankee Doodle*. Happy music, as if the musicians were laughing at me. It was bad enough for Mama to make a fool of herself, but why did she have to drag me down, too? Embarrass me in front of everybody? Did she really resent me being a "big-shot whiz kid"? She'd blamed me for having to come here on my birthday. Maybe she resented ever having me at all.

3
MAMA

★ The tension was a weight bearing down on us in the sultry air. Jackie stomped ahead with his turtle and race car. Mama grumbled that the guard was a modern-day Hitler and she hadn't hurt a soul by taking a little nip. My embarrassment turned into anger. How could she take such a risk as she had today? Did she *want* to lose Jackie and me to a foster home?

The very words made me cringe. I knew foster parents got paid by the state, so I figured strangers who would take in somebody else's kids were only doing it for the money. Patsy McCorkle, a girl I knew in Kansas City, had been in and out of foster homes most of her life, and she'd told stories that would curl your hair.

A gnat buzzed my face and landed on my arm. Angrily, I slapped at it and felt the sting of sunburn that I hadn't noticed before.

It was dusk when we reached our street, and I could barely make out the words on the sign that said, "Dogwood Lane." The streetlight on the pole above it flickered, as if it didn't have the energy to do its job and didn't especially care.

Dogwood Lane was a pretty name, but the street was far from pretty. It was lined on both sides with rundown, crackerbox duplexes with wafer-sized yards. The houses did have porches across the front, though, and in the dim light of early evening, I couldn't see all the patched screens and peeling paint.

I gazed ahead at our duplex, hoping to see a light on in Effie Waisner's side, but her windows were as dark as ours. Please, Effie, I thought, come home soon.

Our half of the porch held an old green upholstered chair that smelled of mice and mildew and had spilled its guts. Effie's half had a swing, where I often sat reading, and flower pots that overflowed with red and pink geraniums that brightened their little corner of the world. Many evenings, Effie and I sat in the swing together, sometimes talking, sometimes not, but always comforted by the clank and creak of the chains.

Just as Effie's porch had a calming effect on me, her personality had a calming effect on Mama. Effie had known Mama since Mama was a little girl, and Effie was the only person she would listen to when she was drinking.

Although our house wasn't locked, Jackie was waiting for Mama and me on the porch, since he was afraid of the dark. As we straggled into the living room, the air slammed into us like a blast furnace.

The house reeked of coffee grounds and onion peels, because the garbage truck had delayed its rounds for the holiday. Dirty dishes and laundry were piled up in the kitchen, waiting for me to clean up the mess. That irritated me, because Mama had been home all morning, while I'd been helping Effie cut out blocks for a quilt. Mama expected me to be the fixer of everything. Call the landlord if the sink gets stopped up. Call him if the rent will be late. Call the factory when she's too hung over to work.

When I turned on the living room light, my trophy glimmered, and I thought gloomily that it was the only thing new and shiny in the place. Behind me, I heard a little splash at the same time Jackie said, "Yuk," and I knew Speedway was relieving himself on the linoleum.

"Put that thing outside," ordered Mama. "I don't want it messing on the couch."

A spot of turtle tinkle couldn't possibly hurt our junk store furniture, but I didn't bring it up. Instead, I said, "Jackie, why don't you play with Speedway on the porch while I fix something to eat?"

He aimed at the front door, slapping at the switch for the porch light on the way. The bulb had burned out a week ago, and he muttered to himself as he stormed outside.

"We need a light bulb," said Mama on her way to the kitchen.

I rolled my eyes and followed her. A light bulb. Something else for me to fix. Pushing aside the clutter in the window above the sink, I made room for my trophy. I frowned when Mama pulled the medicine bottle from her pocket and took a swig.

Her face was red, from either the whiskey or sunburn, and there was a Slushee stain on the front of her dress. "Jackie's mad over that blamed turtle," she said, wiping her mouth. "Are you still mad at me, too?"

"Why shouldn't I be? You embarrassed us both in front of the whole town." I stared at the black specks on the floor where the linoleum had worn away. We didn't have much, but I had my self-respect, and Mama had poked a hole in that today.

"It's the holiday," she said. "I don't like holidays. Too many memories."

Too many memories? Then why in the world had she moved back to Gabriel? Mama's parents and her brother and sister had been killed in a house fire, and except for Jackie and me, she had no family left. It was hard for her on holidays, but it wasn't much fun for us kids, either. The way I saw it, I'd been cheated out of two sets of grandparents—by the fire on Mama's side, and by her secrecy on my father's.

I knew from experience it would be a wasted effort, but I was still angry enough to ask, "Mama, why won't you tell me who my father is?"

The bottle slid from her hand and shattered on the floor, releasing the smell of whiskey. "Now see what you've done," she said, stepping over the shards of glass. "What difference does it make who he is? I've told you before, a dad's not a dad unless he changes diapers, walks the floor, foots the doctor bills. He's not here, never has been, and he's not worth wasting conversation."

"But I—"

"I don't want to talk about it." Mama poured herself a drink from the whiskey bottle under the sink. "Don't count me in for supper. It's too hot to eat," she said and ambled off toward her bedroom.

I shook my head in aggravation. Mama could soak up liquor like sunshine when she was upset, and I knew we were in for a doozy.

After cleaning up the glass, I washed my hands and studied my fingers in the water. They were long and straight, except for my little fingers, which curved outward. "Princess pinkies," Mama called them, because when I drank from a cup, they formed a dainty curl. Dainty, princess, ladylike. The words were light-years away from the real me and the feelings I had inside.

I thought of the frilly pink dress Mama had bought with grocery money, so I'd look nice when I was named top student. She was so determined I was going to be Somebody Someday, and yet she'd been too drunk to attend the awards ceremony.

Jackie came in and stood staring toward Mama's room as he rolled his car back and forth across the table.

"Where's Speedway?" I asked.

"I let him go. He wouldn't do anything but hide in his shell, just like Mama hides in her room."

"Maybe he's tired."

"That's not it," he said grumpily. "He only ran one race. I ran all of them, and *I'm* not a bit tired."

I felt sorry for him. He'd looked forward to the

Fourth of July for weeks, and then in the middle of it, everything went haywire. "Are you hungry?"

"A little."

I fried four hot dogs, burnt black the way he liked them, and added dill pickles to our plates. When we sat down to eat, I said, "After supper, we'll go outside and find a good place to watch the fireworks. I'm sorry I was hateful at the fairgrounds. Mama had a bottle stashed in her pocket, and the security guard was fixing to throw her out. If we hadn't left when we did, she'd have made a terrible scene."

"It's not fair," said Jackie as he crammed a pickle into his mouth.

"I know."

He gazed down the hall again, his face scrunched up from the sour taste. "Why does she have to drink so much?"

I shrugged.

"Is it because Daddy left us?"

"I don't think so. I don't know." Leonard had left three years ago, and I could remember only that there'd been lots of fights, with Mama yelling and Leonard calling her a shrew.

I'd looked up shrew in the dictionary and learned it had two definitions: a mouselike animal, and a scolding, nagging, evil-tempered woman. Except that Leonard had left us in the lurch, I couldn't blame him for taking off like he did. Sometimes I wanted to run away from Mama, too.

My stepfather hadn't been so bad, really. He'd taken us to see the Gateway Arch in St. Louis and the

Swope Park Zoo in Kansas City, and camping every summer at Truman Lake. Now, every once in a while, he sent money and letters to Jackie in envelopes post-marked Idaho. I wondered if he was still with "that woman," as Mama called her—a beauty operator from Lee's Summit.

"Well, if it's not because Daddy left, why is it? There has to be a reason for Mama to keep drinking," said Jackie.

"Maybe it's because of all the sadness in her life. You know she lost her folks in a fire."

"Yeah, but that was a long time ago, before you and I were even born."

"But it left her without any history, sort of. As if she just sprouted up from a seed that was dropped by a bird. You know how it feels to have Leonard gone. Think how it'd be if you didn't have Mama or me, either."

Jackie gazed toward the trophy in the window. "Well, for one thing, I wouldn't have to worry about getting clobbered with a dangerous weapon."

From the teasing look in his eyes, I knew I was forgiven. I chuckled and got up to add our dirty dishes to the pile in the sink. "Let's go out and buy a newspa-per, so I can see my picture."

"But we'll miss the fireworks."

"Not if we get a move on."

We hurried out the back door and three blocks up the alley to the Jiffy Stop, where we bought *The Ga-briel Gazette* from a vending machine on the side-walk. When I opened the paper, I felt my heart swell

with pride. There I was on the front page, receiving
the trophy from Mr. Friendly. The hump on my nose
hardly showed at all.

"Wow!" said Jackie. "How about that?"

Under the picture, in bold-faced type, was the caption, "Freedom reigns on Fourth of July." Below that
were the words, "Rufus Finley presents the winner's
trophy to Freedom Jo Avery at the Independence Day
celebration at the fairgrounds. Freedom, who turned
13 today, spelled down 25 other contestants to win.
She is the daughter of Mary Margaret Ramsdale, 227
Dogwood Lane, Apartment B."

All the way home, I was walking on air.

4

THE STRANGER

★ When I saw the light in our kitchen, I realized that my anger at Mama had melted away. I would have run into her room to show her the paper, but just as we reached the back porch, a distant boom sounded behind us.

"They're starting the fireworks," said Jackie, "and we can't see from here."

He was right. There were too many houses and trees between us and the fairgrounds. I glanced around, looking for a higher spot, and saw Effie's ivy trellis beside her screened-in back porch. "The trellis," I said, keeping my voice low in case Effie had come home while we were gone. "We can climb up and watch from the porch roof."

Jackie scaled up the trellis like a monkey, but I had to remove my shoes and claw my way up barefooted, three toes at a time.

"Come on, Freedom," called Jackie softly from above. "You can see the world from here."

I made out his silhouette perched on the peak of the house roof and scurried up to join him, gripping the gritty shingles with my bare feet. The night seemed darker and more peaceful way up here above the street, away from the yammering of someone's television set.

"Be quiet," I warned. "Mama will break our necks if she knows what we're up to. *If* we don't fall off and beat her to it."

Jackie snickered and took my hand as we heard another boom. A comet whistled upward and exploded into shimmering particles that floated to the earth like fairy dust. "Oh, man," he breathed. "This is neat."

We sat there for several minutes, not making a sound except to "ooh" and "ah" over the light show in the sky.

Eventually, I became aware that what I'd thought was a TV set was a conversation. The voices had grown louder, and I could hear Mama arguing with a man. I inched myself along the peak of the roof to the edge, so I'd be directly above the open window.

". . . living in this hovel," the fellow growled. "Be reasonable."

"Reasonable?" cried Mama. "The time for that is long past. You had no business coming here tonight."

"No business? It certainly is my business!"

"Fourteen years ago, maybe, but not now. Not anymore."

Fourteen years ago? That would have been about the time Mama's folks were killed in the fire. I hugged my knees hard and sat listening with every nerve in my body.

"Look at this place. Look at yourself. What kind of life is—"

"How dare you come here and criticize me, Mr. High and Mighty!"

"What's the matter down there?" whispered Jackie in my ear. "Who's Mama talking to?"

"Sshh," I said. "Just listen."

". . . water under the bridge," the man went on. "Now we've got to talk about—"

"I'm not talking, and I'm not going to listen anymore, either," said Mama, and I could almost see her crossing her arms in defiance. "Get out of my house."

"You haven't changed a bit, have you? You're still letting liquor control you."

"Get out!"

"Mary Margaret, you—"

"You heard me," she shrieked. "Get out!"

"I'll go, but you'll be hearing from me again. When you're sober. Count on it."

I heard a thump-thump, and knew the man was crossing the living room. I swung my legs over to the opposite side of the roof and scooted down the incline on my rump. When I reached the flat roof of the front porch, I lay on my belly and peered below. I could see nothing, except a faint shaft of light from the living room.

The screen door slapped open, and the man's heavy footsteps sounded on the porch, followed by a loud click as Mama flipped at the switch for the porch light. The light didn't work, of course, and everything remained dark below me.

The footsteps stopped as Mama, her voice filled with pure venom, issued a warning. "Don't ever darken my door again, or you'll be sorry. Now get away from here and leave me alone!"

Wordlessly, the man stomped off the porch, and his hulking shadow melted into the night. A few seconds later, a car started up and pulled away, its headlights creating an eerie golden cone on the street.

Finally, I became aware of Jackie's warm breath on my arm.

"Who was that, Freed?" he whispered.

"I don't know. Come on."

We felt our way back up to the peak of the roof. In the night sky over the fairgrounds, a Roman candle whistled upward and burst into a brilliant bouquet.

"Let's go inside," said Jackie. "I'm scared."

"There's nothing to be scared of. That fellow's gone, and Mama's OK." Still, I was frightened myself as we crept down the back side of the roof to our trellis ladder. Could that man have had something to do with the fire that killed Mama's folks? Would he really come back? Was he a threat to Mama?

Jackie scampered down the trellis as if the devil were after him, but I was so shaky, I could barely find the holes for my toes. At last, my feet touched earth. Carrying my shoes and the newspaper, I followed my little brother in the back door.

Mama was sitting at the kitchen table, staring at the glass of whiskey in her hand. I'd expected to see her ranting and throwing things, but she was just slumped over like a droopy doll, looking lonely and defenseless. When she raised her head to stare at us, I saw tears rolling down her cheeks. I wanted to hold her, to protect her, to fix whatever was wrong.

"What's the matter, Mama?" asked Jackie, running to her.

She stroked his fair hair and mumbled, "Where've you been, Cotton Top?"

I envied him for the gentle gesture. Mama seldom touched me at all, unless she was slapping me for smart-mouthing.

"Watching the fireworks."

"We heard a man in here," I said. "Who was it?"

"No one important."

"How can you say that? He made you cry."

Mama swiped at her tears. "He just dredged up the past. It's nothing to worry about. . . . I've got a splitting headache. I think I'll go to bed." She stood up, still holding her drink.

I suspected if she left now without giving me some answers, I'd never find out what was going on. Stalling for time, I held out the paper and said, "Wait, Mama. Look at this."

She stared at my picture on the front page as if she were seeing a ghost, and in her mind, I guess she was. "The look on your face," she said as she touched my image on the paper, "it's exactly like Josie Ann's, when she got that bike for Christmas."

Josie Ann was Mama's younger sister who'd burned to death. She'd been gone for fourteen years. Why was Mama talking about her now?

I folded the paper, being careful not to crease my

picture. "I'll go to the junk store tomorrow and get a frame," I said. "Then we can hang this on the wall."

"No!" said Mama.

"Why?"

"I don't want to have to look at it every day. It would be a constant reminder. . . ." Her voice trailed off, and she didn't finish the sentence.

I couldn't believe it—my own mother telling me she couldn't stand to look at my picture. "For somebody who's so unimportant," I said, "that guy sure put you in a rotten mood."

"I told you not to worry about it."

"But I *am* worried. It sounded like he's going to make trouble."

Mama was unsteady on her feet from the liquor, but her blue eyes flashed with anger. "Freedom Avery, you had no business eavesdropping on a private conversation."

"We weren't eavesdropping on purpose. We were up on the roof and couldn't help but hear."

She must have missed the part about the roof, because she said, "Well, it's my business, and I don't want you meddling in it!" After draining her glass, she stormed off down the hall. She came back for the whiskey bottle, retraced her steps, and slammed the door to her room.

The whole bottle. And there was nothing I could do to stop her.

I wished Effie were home, but I knew she wasn't yet. Our walls were practically cardboard, and if somebody blinked on our side, Effie knew it. If she'd heard

Mama and that fellow arguing, she'd have come to investigate. Maybe it was just as well, though, because of her bad heart.

"Freed?" said Jackie, moving over close to me. "What if that guy comes back?"

I put my arm around him and felt him trembling. "Then he'll have to take on the three of us. We're a family, Cotton Top, and we stick together." Jumping into what I hoped was a karate stance, I started chopping the air with my hands. "Yee-ha! Take that and that and *that*."

"You look like a broken windmill," giggled Jackie.

"So I'm not into Japanese defense. I'm more into Chinese water torture. It's time for you to get in the tub, little bro, and scrape off some of that grime from the fairgrounds."

Jackie glanced toward the black hallway. "Will you turn on the light?"

Are other kids his age so afraid of the dark? I wondered as I turned on the light in the bathroom and accompanied him to our bedroom while he got clean clothes. I liked the dark. In Kansas City, I'd spent hours on the balcony of our apartment at night, gazing toward downtown where skyscrapers shone like miniature flashlights in the sky. I hoped Jackie would outgrow his fear of darkness soon. I didn't want other kids to find his weak spot, the way Laura Nell had found mine.

While Jackie splashed in the tub, I washed the dishes. Instead of propping up a book to read as I worked, I just stared at my spelling trophy. "Knowledge Is Freedom," it said, but I, the champion speller, felt empty, inadequate, shackled by so much I didn't know. I was supposed to be so good at fixing everything, but I didn't know how to protect Mama from a stranger she wouldn't talk about. Didn't know how to fix her drinking problem. Didn't know how to make her tell me who my father was.

When the dishes were done, I carried the trophy to the bedroom and placed it on the bookshelf, beside the books I'd bought at the junk store. Then I sat down on my bed to read some more of *Across Five Aprils,* a novel Alice had loaned me about the Civil War.

A few minutes later, Jackie came into our room yawning, his face freckled with beads of moisture from the steamy bathroom. "I'm tired," he said, "but it's too hot to sleep."

I folded down his covers. "Give it a try. You've had a rough day."

As he crawled into bed, he asked, "Are you gonna stay in here?"

"No. I need a bath, too."

"Then don't turn off the light."

"I won't," I promised and bent to kiss him goodnight.

"I'm afraid I'll have bad dreams."

"Think about happy things, like playing with Mike or seeing the animals at the zoo."

Jackie chuckled. "Remember that elephant the time we ran out of peanuts?"

"Aaack! Yes. He stuck his slobbery old trunk right

on my face. I hope that's the last kiss I ever get from an elephant."

Jackie laughed and rolled over, and before I could gather up my nightgown and underwear, he was dead to the world.

I took a good long soak in the tub, hoping to unwind enough to sleep. When I finished in the bathroom, I left the light on for Jackie and went to our room. His breathing was slow and even, and I knew he wasn't having bad dreams.

I crawled into my bed and rolled over on my stomach. My body prickled from sunburn, and trickles of sweat made me itch. Slipping one arm underneath the mattress, I moved it steadily back and forth to feel the coolness between the mattress and box springs. It was a nervous habit, like popping my knuckles, only no one ever complained.

Eventually, I punched up my pillow and changed my position. In the stillness, I could hear the wall clock in the kitchen. Tick-tock, tick-tock. When I at last fought my way to sleep, I dreamed the clock was a bomb waiting to blast our world to smithereens.

5

THE BINGE

★ The grinding and chugging of our neighbor's old pickup woke me up early. That, and seeing *The Gabriel Gazette* on the dresser, made me grumpy. It wasn't my fault that my picture reminded Mama of Josie Ann.

In the bathroom, I frowned at my reflection in the mirror. My eyes were ringed with dark circles, accenting those hideous freckles and that camel's hump of a nose.

Mama's door was open a few inches, and I peeked in at her. She was lying crossways on the covers, face down, still wearing that checkered sundress. Her hair had fallen out of its pony tail and was splayed out like a dirty dish towel across the bedspread. The whiskey bottle on the floor was half empty, and its stench permeated the room. This was a full-scale binge, for sure.

Shaking my head, I backed out and closed the door. In a little while, I'd use Effie's phone to call the factory and tell them the same old fib: "Mary Margaret Ramsdale is sick and won't be in today."

Money would really be tight next week. The Fourth of July had fallen on a Wednesday, and the rule at the factory was that you had to work the day before and the day after to get paid for a holiday. Mama would lose out for the Fourth. We were already behind on the rent, and if she kept this up, we'd be out in the street.

Mama was too proud to take a penny from me. I'd saved most of the money I'd earned baby-sitting for Bonnie Rivers's two little boys while she sang at a club on Friday and Saturday nights. A hundred and twenty-one dollars seemed like a fortune to me, but it wouldn't have caught us up on the rent.

The garbage was ripe, so I hauled the bags off the back porch and dropped them at the curb. When I saw Effie's garbage out, I knew she had come home.

In the kitchen again, I poured the last of the milk over a bowl of Cheerios. Automatically, I rinsed out the jug, filled it with water, and carried it to the deep freeze that had been left on the back porch by a previous tenant. The deep freeze was rusty and had a noisy, grumbling motor, but we'd been using it since the freezer on our refrigerator quit working. There wasn't much in it now, except some leftover chili, three ice cube trays, and about two dozen gallon jugs of ice. "It costs too much to run an empty freezer," Mama said, so we were filling it up with ice.

I ate my breakfast in the living room and tried to read, but I couldn't concentrate. I was worried about Mama. What awful things in her past periodically drove her to drink herself into a stupor?

She'd been happy with Leonard for a while, and I thought she must have been happy as a girl, judging by the picture in her senior yearbook. In that photo, she was beautiful, with honey-colored hair, creamy skin, and deep-set blue eyes that seemed to look right into my own.

Mama wouldn't let me browse through the yearbook, but sometimes, when she was tipsy enough to be cheerful, she'd show it to me herself. The cheerfulness never lasted long. She'd tell me that the yearbook had survived because it was in a friend's car the night her folks' house burned, and then she'd start crying and dripping tears on the pages.

"We're out of milk," said Jackie in my ear.

"Oh! You scared me," I said as my hand flew to my chest.

He didn't smile, and his blue eyes were rimmed with dark circles like mine. Maybe he hadn't slept as well as I'd thought.

"I wanted Cheerios, but the milk's gone."

"I know. I'm sorry. I'll borrow some from Effie."

Still in my nightgown, I grabbed an empty jar from the kitchen, then padded barefoot out the back door and up onto Effie's porch. Through the screen, I could see Effie, her shaggy white head bent over a newspaper. She was wearing her faded pink bathrobe, and her lumpy feet were crammed into navy blue house slippers that had cutouts for her bunions. She looked old and wrinkled and comfortable, like broken-in leather.

"Knock, knock," I said as I opened the screen door

and walked into the aroma of coffee and scrambled eggs. On the table lay a rainbow of pieces I'd cut for a Buzz Saw quilt, and a stack of blocks Effie'd sewn together by hand.

"The devil must have passed over somebody's grave, child. I was just reading about you, and here you are," she said, smiling a toothless grin and reaching into her pocket for her teeth.

"I came to borrow some milk and to use your phone."

Effie's smile faded as she slipped her teeth into her mouth. "Mary Margaret's at it again?"

I nodded.

"Mercy me," sighed Effie. She glanced at the ceiling and shook her head. "What was it this time?"

"She got caught drinking at the fairgrounds. Then last night, some guy came to the house and got her all riled up."

"About what?"

"I don't know. She wouldn't say."

"Demons from the past," said Effie, almost to herself. "Well, go ahead and make your call. I'll come over and check on her when I get dressed."

I fingered a quilt block. Its center yellow square was surrounded by brown and yellow triangles that represented saw teeth. It looked like a sun to me. "Effie," I said, trying to sound casual, "what do you know about the fire that killed Mama's folks?"

"Nothing except what I saw in the papers. There was an explosion of some kind. Mary Margaret's parents burned to death in the prime of life, and her brother and sister, too. Worst accident in Gabriel's history."

"It was an accident for sure?"

"Why, yes, far as I know. Why?"

"No reason. I—Mama never talks about it, and I'm curious."

"She never has been able to talk about it, and that's a shame. It would have helped her deal with her grief. She went a little bit crazy there for a while and hit the bottle hard. Couldn't accept the fact that it happened. Sometimes, I think she hasn't accepted it yet, and that's why she goes off the deep end with her liquor."

"You'd think, after fourteen years, she'd begin to get over it," I said, unable to keep the bitterness from my voice.

Effie got up and placed her hands on my shoulders. Her eyes were bright as coals in her wrinkled face. "Don't be too hard on your mother. There's an old Indian saying, 'Don't judge a man until you've walked a mile in his moccasins.' When I lost my Vincel, I learned about the pain of death, but even I can't imagine the agony of losing four loved ones at once. Why do you think Mary Margaret moved back to Gabriel? To be close to the Avery graves."

I was ashamed when she said that. Mama would have been eighteen when her folks died. Nineteen when I was born. It must have been scary, having a baby but no husband. No family at all. Just Effie. A thought struck me like an electrical shock. "Effie," I asked, scarcely daring to breathe, "do you know who my father is?"

Her teeth clicked as she shook her head. "No, child. I knew there'd come a day when you'd ask me that, but I honestly don't know. It wasn't my place to be asking such things. I was a friend of Mary Margaret's, not her judge."

I called the factory, borrowed the milk and delivered it to Jackie, then went back outside and sat on the porch steps. Effie'd helped me see Mama's drinking in a different light. It was a sickness, brought on by the death of her family and complicated by me, who'd probably been a cranky, squalling baby, considering how bullheaded I was now. Maybe I was the reason she still drank. I made a promise to do better, to try and please her. I couldn't change the past and bring Mama's family back, but I could change myself. I'd stop being stubborn and mouthy. I'd stop griping about the work I had to do around the house. I'd do the laundry, just as soon as I got dressed.

In the bathroom, I washed my face and sprayed on deodorant, then pulled on a yellow tank top and yesterday's cutoffs with six quarters still in the pocket. I was tying my hair back into a pony tail when Effie "yoo-hooed" at the back door.

I heard her speak to Jackie, and heard her slow, shuffling steps as she came down the hall to check on Mama. Seconds later, she yelled, "Freedom! Help! Call an ambulance!"

I dashed out the door and collided with Jackie as he burst into the hall from the kitchen. We both bounced off a wall and kept running toward Mama's room.

Effie was on the bed on her knees, slapping Mama

on the cheek and shaking her by the shoulder. Mama didn't respond. Her face and arms were all splotchy, and one hand dangled limply over the edge of the bed.

"Mama!" I cried, grabbing that hand for dear life. It was cold as ice. Then I saw something on the night stand that made me cold, too—Mama's sleeping pill container with the lid off.

"Call the ambulance," said Effie. "Hurry! She's still breathing, but just barely."

I whirled around so fast, I got dizzy and crashed into the door facing on the way out. I sailed through the house and off the back porch without touching the steps, flew into Effie's kitchen, and snatched the telephone receiver from its hook. My hands were shaking as I dialed the emergency number posted on the wall. Someone answered on the first ring, and I yelped, "My mother's unconscious. Send an ambulance to two twenty-seven Dogwood Lane, Apartment B."

"Right away," said a woman dispatcher. "Don't hang up." I heard her repeat what I'd said to someone before she got back to me. "Now, tell me your name and the nature of the problem."

"My name's Freedom Avery. My mother is Mary Margaret Ramsdale. She's all blotchy and cold, and we can't wake her up."

"Has she had this trouble before?"

"No! Not like this!"

"Has she been taking any medication?"

"She had a headache last night. I think she took some sleeping pills." I was afraid the dispatcher would stop the ambulance if she knew about the whiskey, so I didn't mention that.

"Is someone with her now? An adult?"

"Effie is. Our neighbor."

"Good. Then you go out front and flag down the ambulance. It should be there in three or four minutes. We'll need the pill container, so the doctor will know what he's dealing with."

"OK," I said and slammed down the receiver. When I got back home, Effie was still trying to rouse Mama, while Jackie stood wide-eyed and silent at the foot of the bed.

"They'll be here in a couple of minutes," I said. "They want somebody to watch for them out front."

"I'll go," said Jackie.

I let him, knowing he needed something important to do. I snatched up the container of pills and breathed a prayer of gratitude that it was almost full. At least, Mama hadn't deliberately tried to harm herself.

After fetching a wet washcloth, I bathed her face and tried to wipe the Slushee stain off the front of her dress.

"Don't worry about that, hon," said Effie gently. "They've seen worse."

I swallowed back tears and kept dabbing at the stain. Mama wouldn't want to go to the hospital in a dirty dress. When the stain was gone, I got rid of the whiskey bottle, too.

After what seemed like an hour, the ambulance arrived and the attendants came rushing in behind Jackie. I saw the look that passed between them when they began helping Mama, and I knew they smelled the alcohol in the room.

✦

Only one of us could ride in the ambulance with Mama, so Effie offered to stay behind with Jackie. I jumped in the front seat and fastened my safety belt when the driver asked, but I rode sideways and kept my eyes on Mama in the back. The attendant was giving her oxygen and checking her vital signs.

When we reached the hospital, Mama was wheeled into the emergency room. I tried to follow, but a woman stopped me to get all the particulars. I stared at her name tag—Mrs. Dorcas Tuttle—as I told her Mama's name, age, social security number, and place of employment, and said that we had insurance through the shoe factory.

Mrs. Tuttle recorded all that on a form, then asked, "Next of kin?"

Next of kin? I thought that was what you needed when people died. Did that mean it was too late for Mama? I spun around and looked at her stretcher. She was surrounded by men in white, and it didn't appear that they'd given up on her yet.

"Next of kin?" repeated Mrs. Tuttle.

"I guess that's me," I croaked. "I'm her daughter."

"And your name?"

"Freedom Jo Avery."

"Is there someone you'd like me to notify? Your father, maybe, or your grandparents?"

My father was nameless. My grandparents were dead. "No, thank you," I murmured. "I'll call home when I know something."

"There's a waiting room around the corner. I'll come and get you after a while."

"Could—could I please sit there?" I asked, indicating a wheelchair by the counter. "I promise to stay out of the way."

Mrs. Tuttle must have read the anxiety in my face. She smiled and nodded. "I'm really too busy filing to see who's sitting where."

I dropped into the wheelchair and sat staring into the emergency room. My head was throbbing, as if little lumberjacks were splitting logs inside it. A whole list of regrets sifted through my mind. I was sorry for every complaint, every hateful word, every intolerant thought regarding Mama. I renewed my promise to try harder to please her. If she pulled through.

A gagging sound interrupted my musing, and I saw Mama's legs jerk.

"Quick! The bowl!" someone said, and I realized Mama was throwing up. It was the sweetest sound I'd ever heard.

"She's lucky," said a bald-headed man. "Barbiturates and alcohol make a deadly combination."

A few minutes later, he came walking toward me, and I leaped from the chair. "Is everything all right?"

"I'm Doctor Rhiner. Are you here with Mrs. Ramsdale?"

"Yes, I'm her daughter. How is she?"

"Your mother had a reaction to her sleeping pills, possibly because she'd consumed so much liquor that her blood-alcohol content was incredibly high. We're going to keep her overnight for observation. How long had she been drinking?"

"All night, I think."

Doctor Rhiner's polished skull reflected the overhead light as he shook his head. "Well, fortunately, she took only a few pills. If she'd swallowed many more, I don't think we could have saved her."

"Will she be all right?"

"This time, yes. But I'm going to refer her to a counselor. See if we can prevent an episode like this from happening again."

Behind the doctor, the men were lifting Mama onto a different bed. "Could I see her?" I asked.

He glanced back and called, "Ralph, what room is she going to?"

"Three-fourteen."

Doctor Rhiner said to me, "Give them a few minutes to get her situated. It's not visiting hours yet, but I'll speak to the charge nurse. Don't be surprised if your mother's too sleepy to talk. She's still got a lot of junk in her bloodstream."

The doctor left, and I sank back into the wheelchair. My legs didn't want to hold me up. When I'd gathered my strength, I asked Mrs. Tuttle if I could call home.

She winked at me and replied, "I'm really too busy to see who's using the phone."

I gave her a feeble smile and dialed Effie's number. After telling Effie how Mama was, I said, "I'm going to stay with her a little while."

"OK, but don't stay too long. There's a little fellow here who needs a big sister to lean on."

"Tell him to hang in there. Mama's going to be just fine."

I hung up the phone and took the elevator to the third floor. When I entered Mama's room and saw her in a hospital gown with an IV attached to her arm, I had to fight back tears. Her complexion, instead of being splotchy, was a sickly gray. The veins showed in her eyelids, reminding me of a newly hatched chicken I'd seen once at a farm.

Cautiously, I touched her hand, which felt wonderfully warm. "Mama," I whispered. "It's me. How do you feel?"

Her eyes fluttered open, then closed. "Josie Ann?"

"No, Mama. It's Freedom."

She smiled without opening her eyes.

I wanted to hug her and plant a kiss on her forehead, but I held back. It would have seemed like stealing, since she wasn't awake enough to know what I was doing.

The bed next to Mama's was empty, so I walked across the room and stood gazing out the window. In the distance, the headstones in the cemetery looked like Chiclets. I remembered Decoration Day, when Mama'd driven Jackie and me out there to put flowers on her folks' graves. She'd cried that day and gotten drunk that night and thrown a bottle at two cats fighting in the alley. Miss Harbaugh from the Child Protection Agency had shown up the next morning to investigate a complaint.

Shaking off that memory, I tried to find the exact spot where Mama's family was buried. There had been shade trees and an angel statue near the Avery monument.

Avery. It had given me a chill to see my own name on a tombstone, and the chill had settled into a little knot of shame. Avery was Mama's maiden name, chiseled in granite—a declaration forever that she hadn't married my father.

I wondered if Josie Ann had known my dad, and whether she would tell me about him, if she were here today. I hadn't known Josie Ann or her brother or my grandparents, and Mama seldom talked about them. That's why I'd been so surprised last night when she said I reminded her of her sister. Maybe I should have coaxed Mama into telling me about her family. Maybe it would have eased her pain.

In the cemetery, the shiny black cars of a funeral procession made their way to an open grave. Beetles parading to an anthill. I stared, mesmerized, reliving the fear I'd felt when I thought Mama was going to die. Then, with a shudder, I yanked the draperies closed and went back to sit with Mama. I hoped, when she woke up, she wouldn't take a notion to look out the window.

6

NO PROMISES

★ I hiked toward home, and was I ever working up a sweat by the time I got to Hackberry Street. The thermometer at the bank said it was ninety-five degrees, but it had to be hotter than that. I could have baked a cake on the sidewalk.

The rusty sign at Second Time Around was creaking on its hinges. I jingled the quarters in my pocket and decided to stop in and pick up a used toy or something for Jackie. He'd had his eye on a wagon, but I couldn't afford that. The poor kid. He'd been like a lost puppy the past three years. He depended on me a lot, but I knew I could never take up all the slack left by Mama's drinking and Leonard's leaving. Things would get better, though, because I was going to work on making Mama happy.

When I saw my reflection in the window, it dawned on me that everything I was wearing had come from the junk store. Even my cutoffs had once been a pair of bell-bottomed jeans. Too out of date to be Lydia's rejects.

I studied the new display of old camping gear in the

window—an army tent, cots, a campstove, an enamel coffee pot, an aluminum cookset.

The gear reminded me of my stepfather and the times he'd taken us camping at Truman Lake. I wondered idly if he'd taken his lady friend camping in Idaho, and if he ever felt guilty about leaving his little boy behind. Jackie was eight now, a good age to appreciate camping out.

I looked at the cookset again—cups and plates and a skillet nestled inside a kettle. I couldn't take Jackie camping, but I could take him the cookset. He and his friend, Mike, who had a U.S. Army canteen, were forever playing soldiers on the march. If Jackie owned the cookset, they could have a regular bivouac.

The cookset cost two dollars, according to the price tag. I could probably get it for the dollar and a half I had in my pocket. Henry Bockelman hated to lose a sale.

I armed myself with a good, deep breath, pushed open the door, and went inside. A mixture of smells closed in on me—mothballs, dust, musty furniture, and sweat. The sweat, I knew, came from Henry, who had just about everything here but deodorant.

The floor of the junk store alternately sagged and buckled, giving me the sensation that I was looking at it through an antique mirror. The cluttered aisles were hazardous, and the whole store was lit by only six bare bulbs dangling from a twelve-foot ceiling.

Henry was sprawled in a recliner, cleaning his ears as he listened to country music on the radio and soaked up the breeze from a fan. Being downwind, I caught a good whiff of him and wondered how any-body who sat around all day could sweat so hard.

When Henry realized he had a customer, he heaved himself from the chair and stuck the toothpick end of the ear spoon into his mouth. "Hello there, Freedom. What're you gonna beat me out of today?"

"Hi, Henry." I pointed to the window, saying, "I'd like to see that aluminum cookset."

"Sure thing, sweet thing," he replied with a wink.

I kept my distance from him as he came around the counter and sauntered up the aisle.

Henry climbed into the window and picked his way around the tent. "Going camping with the Boy Scouts?" he asked, backing out with the cookset and handing it to me. "Or just scouting for a boy?"

I shrugged and examined the cookset.

"It's a steal at two dollars."

"I don't know," I hedged. "It's dented up pretty bad, and this pan is burned black on the bottom."

"Well, what do you expect for two bucks?"

"Something better than this." I handed him the cookset and started toward the door. This was the part Henry hated.

"Well, now, just hold your horses, little lady. What'll you give for it?"

I turned and looked back over my shoulder. "A dollar."

"A dollar and a half."

"Sold." I walked toward Henry, fishing the six quarters out of my shorts pocket.

"Freedom Avery, you drive a hard bargain."

I grinned at him and slapped the quarters into his palm, then snatched up the cookset and left.

✦

Dogwood Lane looked quiet and bleached out, except for Effie's geraniums along our sidewalk. I headed straight for her front door, where the music blaring from the "Beverly Hillbillies" told me Jackie was watching television.

I stepped into the living room and stood blinking at the sudden change from sunlight. The air was only slightly cooler than the oven outside, but it smelled like chocolate.

"Freed!" said Jackie. "How's Mama?"

"She's gonna be fine, Cotton Top." My eyes adjusted to the dimness of the room, and I saw him lying on the floor. "I brought you something."

He jumped up and grabbed the cookset. "Wow! It looks like genuine army gear!"

While he was examining it, Effie came in from the kitchen. She was wearing a bib apron over her plaid housedress, and her socks were sagging around the tops of her tennis shoes. "You look hot as a firecracker," she said. "Wash up, and we'll eat, and you can tell us all about your mama. I fixed a big pitcher of lemonade."

"Sounds good." In the bathroom, I helped myself to Effie's deodorant, splashed cold water on my face, and frowned at the new freckles that had popped out on my nose.

I went to the kitchen, where a rickety fan was clattering in the window and a chocolate layer cake with fudge icing sat on the stovetop. Jackie was filling glasses with lemonade, while Effie was arranging sandwiches on a plate.

"What can I do?" I asked, realizing that I had an enormous appetite.

"Just sit down," said Effie as she pulled out a chair and sat down herself.

When Jackie and I were seated, she asked the blessing, then passed around the sandwiches and said, "OK, let's hear about Mary Margaret."

I told them everything, except the part about Mama throwing up, and finished by saying, "While he's got her in the hospital, Doctor Rhiner's going to call in a counselor. To talk to her about her drinking."

"Well, we can pray that does some good," Effie said.

I swallowed a bite of bologna and cheese. "I don't think it will. We've all tried talking before."

"Yes, but this time she almost died. I imagine that'll scare her into doing something different."

"I hope you're right."

"I wish Daddy was here," said Jackie. "I'll bet he could stop her from drinking."

"I don't know about that," replied Effie. "It has to come from inside a person. That's one decision Mary Margaret will have to make for herself."

"What's so great about drinking, anyway?" asked Jackie.

Effie shrugged. "They say alcoholism is a disease, but it's the only disease I ever heard of that comes out of a bottle." She looked thoughtful for a minute before going on. "My Vincel was a drinker, right up till the day he died."

I hadn't known that, but it explained why Effie understood Mama so well.

"Toward the end, he couldn't even go to the bathroom by himself. Our son made noises about putting him in a rest home. I told him he wasn't taking care of his daddy—I was—and I wouldn't listen to any more talk like that. Makes me think he'll want to put me away when I get old." She gave a little snort and added, "That'll be the day. I'd shrivel up and die first, like the grass beneath the whipping post on my grand-daddy's farm."

"Whipping post?" I said.

"Yes. Back before the Civil War, the man who owned the land had slaves. The post where he whipped them is still standing, but the grass won't grow at all. I always thought it was nature's way of showing that one person ought never to lay claim against another."

I got up to cut the cake. My fingers were gooey with chocolate when someone knocked at the front door. Effie went to answer it, while I washed my hands and set our dessert on the table.

"Sorry to bother you," said the visitor, "but I heard voices, and I thought I might find Mrs. Ramsdale here."

The person speaking was Hilda Harbaugh from the Child Protection Agency, and I was no longer interested in cake. Why had she come today? Surely she hadn't already heard that Mama was sick.

"She's not here, but the kids are," replied Effie.

"Where's Mrs. Ramsdale?"

I shot a glance at Jackie and saw the troubled look on his face. He got up and took my hand, and together we crept into the living room.

Miss Harbaugh was on the porch, and I glared at her through the screen. Her hair gleamed like steel wool in the sunlight, and her beefy body with its huge, jutting bosom gave her the appearance of a Kool-Aid pitcher with legs.

". . . in the hospital?" she was saying. "Was she hurt in a fight last night? Someone called this morning and reported a disturbance."

The busybody neighbor had reported us again.

Effie sighed. "You'd better talk to Freedom," she said, opening the door to invite the social worker in.

Miss Harbaugh bustled inside, one arm clutching a briefcase that matched her lizard-gray suit and clod-hopper shoes. "Hello, children. What's wrong with your mother?" she said, sinking down on the couch.

I sat across from her in the overstuffed chair, and Jackie crowded in beside me. Effie perched on the chair's arm. It was going to be three against one.

"Mama had a reaction to her sleeping pills," I said.

"Sleeping pills?"

I stared at my feet and nodded.

"Was she, by any chance, drinking when she took the pills?"

I nodded again.

Miss Harbaugh reached into her briefcase for our file and a notebook and wrote something down. "What's the name of her physician?" she asked.

"Doctor Rhiner. He's keeping her in the hospital for observation."

"Mrs. Waisner, I assume the children are staying with you?"

"This is their second home," said Effie.

"They're fortunate to have you. Now," said Miss Harbaugh, turning her attention back to me, "did Doctor Rhiner give any indication of how long Mrs. Ramsdale will be in the hospital?"

"Just overnight." I craned my neck to see as the social worker scrawled something else, but I couldn't read her writing upside down.

Miss Harbaugh covered the paper with her hand. "Mrs. Waisner, if Mrs. Ramsdale would agree, how would you feel about keeping the children for an extended period? Say thirty days?"

"Thirty—? I don't understand. Freedom just told you, Mary Margaret will be home in a day or two."

"This is the fourth time someone has registered a complaint against Mrs. Ramsdale. I'm going to suggest she go away for treatment."

"Go away?" I gulped.

"There's a hospital in the city that specializes in treating alcohol abuse. It has a very high success rate."

"But we can't— She can't— She can't afford to miss work," I said.

"She can't afford to keep drinking. It's dangerous to mix any drug with alcohol."

I stared at my shoes again. Forcing Mama to go away for treatment wouldn't work. Hadn't Effie just said that decision had to come from within herself?

Miss Harbaugh said, "Your mother probably has accumulated sick leave, and some insurance companies pay for alcohol abuse treatment. It's worth checking into. I'll go see her first thing in the morning."

"What if she won't do it?" I asked.

"I think she will, once she understands that it will preserve the family unit in the long run."

I squinted at her and tried to figure this out. Before, Miss Harbaugh had talked about a foster home. Now it sounded like she wanted to keep our family together.

"Mrs. Waisner," she asked, "how old are you?"

"Seventy-three."

"Are you in good health?"

"I—uh—had a heart attack this spring, but I'm on medication and I'm fine now."

Miss Harbaugh frowned. "Perhaps I spoke out of turn about your caring for the children. It would be stressful, and we wouldn't want to jeopardize your health."

"Freedom and Jackie are good kids. They wouldn't be any trouble."

I wasn't sure Miss Harbaugh would believe her, since somewhere in that file was a report that said Mama had slapped me for being a smart-mouth.

"Well, we'll see," said the social worker, putting her things back in her briefcase and zipping it shut. "I'll talk to Mrs. Ramsdale and my supervisor and see what we can work out."

"What'll happen to the kids if I can't keep them?" asked Effie.

"There are three options. One, sending them to a

relative or friend. Two, sending them to the juvenile justice center for—"

"The juvenile justice center?" cried Effie.

"Hold on. There's a misconception that the center is only for juvenile delinquents. It also takes in children who haven't done anything wrong, but have had to be removed from troubled homes."

It sounded like jail to me. I tried to swallow and couldn't. Knowing the answer before I asked the question, I squeaked, "What's the third option?"

"Foster care. Our foster homes are full at the moment, although we've got some families in training. Until they're approved, we'd have to send you to another county. Maybe even separate homes."

"You can't do that," I said, slipping an arm around Jackie.

"We want to stay with Effie," he said. "She's like our grandma."

"I'll see what I can do, but I'll make no promises."

7
KNIGHT IN SHINING ARMOR

None of us spoke as we stood at the door and watched Miss Harbaugh drive away.

Finally, when the car turned the corner and disappeared, Effie said, "My chest hurts. Indigestion. I'm going to stretch out on the couch."

I searched her face, looking for some sign that her old heart could stand the strain of having Jackie and me underfoot for a whole month. All I saw were troubled eyes and wrinkles.

When Effie almost sat on Jackie's cookset, she asked, "Where'd that come from?"

"Freedom brought it to me," he said, retrieving it. "Is it OK if I play with Mike?"

"Sure, hon. Just stay in the neighborhood and come when I call."

I wandered into the kitchen where our dessert sat untouched on the table. As I covered the cake with waxed paper and washed the dishes, I thought about what would happen if Mama went away and Jackie and I couldn't stay with Effie.

There weren't any relatives to take us. If I spent a

month in the juvenile justice center, I'd be branded "Jailbird Avery." The only other option was a foster home. Or homes.

A picture of Patsy McCorkle popped into my mind. Patsy was the girl in Kansas City who'd spent most of her twelve years in foster homes. Some were good, and some were bad, but it was the bad ones I remembered.

At the age of seven, Patsy had received a worn-out doll on Christmas morning, while her foster parents' own children got new toys and games and clothes. Two years later, she'd been a built-in maid and baby-sitter for a different foster mother, who ruled the house with an iron hand.

But the place Patsy was living when I last saw her was the worst of all. Her foster father was always touching her and trying to kiss her. When Patsy went to bed at night, she barricaded the door with a broom crammed down behind the dresser, so he'd have to break the handle to get in. "I thought I heard it crack one night and woke up screaming," Patsy told me, "but it was only the crash of thunder from a storm."

When I asked why she didn't report the creep, Patsy replied, "Are you kidding? And take the chance that I'll get sent to someplace worse? His wife is kind-hearted and decent and makes me feel like somebody special."

Maybe Patsy was just unlucky. Maybe not. But I'd learned enough about foster homes to never want to go to one.

After rinsing out the sink and drying my hands, I

headed for the living room to talk to Effie, but found her snoozing away on the couch. Since her teeth were out, her breath was coming out in a whistle.

I went next door to our house, hooked the water hose to the sink, and started filling the wringer washer on the back porch. While I did the laundry, I tried to sort out the confusion in my mind. I wanted Mama to stop drinking, but I didn't want her to go away to do it, especially if it meant Jackie and I would be farmed out to another county. Why couldn't Miss Harbaugh just leave us alone and let us live our lives?

In frustration, I kicked the empty clothes basket halfway across the yard.

✦

Effie was watching a game show and laying out quilt blocks on the coffee table. When I walked in, she said, "What do you think, child? Do all these different colors hurt your eyes?"

Tilting my head, I studied the busy design. "No. With a name like Buzz Saw, it ought to be wild."

"Wild? I don't want to scandalize the ladies in the guild."

"They'll be impressed, buzzing about it for weeks."

Effie missed my joke. "I don't know," she said absently as she rearranged a few blocks. "Some of those women spend a fortune, buying color-coordinated fabric. I've got to use whatever's on sale."

"Trust me, Effie, it's going to look great. Would you mind if I went over to Alice's for a while?"

"No. Just watch out for strangers."

I smiled at her. Effie had this wild notion that every man was a maniac out to kidnap girls. "I promise not to hitch a ride unless the guy's got a white hat and a Bible."

"Freedom!"

"Just wanted to see if you were listening," I said. "You know I wouldn't hitchhike."

"I know that, or I wouldn't let you out of the house. Now get on out of here and let me go color blind in peace."

By the time I got to Alice's house on Birch Street, I was seeing yellow dots on everything because of the heat. Her front door was open, but the house was graveyard quiet. I knocked anyway, deciding that if no one was home, I'd get a drink at the faucet on the side of the house.

I heard a little thump and footsteps and peered through the screen to see a grinning Alice with watery eyes.

"Well, pass the spit can, Willie! Look who's here!" she said as she flung open the door. She was wearing a lime green, one-piece job that made her look like a giant green bean, and in her hand was a book I'd loaned her, *The Count of Monte Cristo.*

I stepped inside and fanned my face. "Forget the spit can. I'm so dry I don't have any spit. You got anything to drink?"

"Tina's got some monster punch with berry blood, or I could make some Kool-Aid."

"I'll take the Kool-Aid," I said, blinking away the vision of Miss Harbaugh, the Kool-Aid pitcher with legs. "That is, if your mom won't care that I just dropped in."

"She took Tina to the dentist, but she wouldn't mind anyway," said Alice as she led the way to the kitchen. "You know Mom. Give her some scissors and a needle and thread, and she wouldn't care if we burned the house down."

Although Alice's mother worked part-time, she was organized. Her home was clean and neat, except for the corner of the kitchen that held her sewing machine. Threads and bits of fabric cluttered the floor, and swatches of material printed with palm trees and purple parrots were scattered across the table. Adding to the mess were Tina's Barbie dolls.

Alice laid the book on the counter and cleared off a place at the table, saying, "Mom's making me a new jump suit."

"That's nice." Inwardly, I winced. It was a jump suit all right. I'd jump off a cliff if I had to wear it.

"Don't lie to me," said Alice. "You wouldn't wear it to a dog fight."

I grinned at her and thumbed through the book, thinking how our love of reading was what had thrown us together in the first place. When I'd volunteered to help out in the school library, Alice had shown me the ropes.

"Bottoms up," she said, handing me a glass of grape Kool-Aid. She turned on the window fan and sat down at the table.

I sat across from her, sipping my drink and listening as the air rustled the tissue paper of the jump suit pattern. I knew Alice was planning to take home ec this fall, and I wondered if she'd end up sewing furiously like her mother. Probably, I thought, and that scared me. What if I took up drinking like Mama?

"Is my Kool-Aid that bad?" asked Alice. "You're frowning like I'd sweetened it with arsenic."

I dragged my attention back to her and told her everything that had happened since I'd last seen her at the fairgrounds.

When I was finished, Alice gave a low whistle. "Boy, if the Child Protection Agency won't let you stay with Effie, you're in for a plethora of trouble. Don't you have any relatives anywhere?"

"Jackie's got grandparents in Kansas City, but they're in senior housing. Besides, they wouldn't want me. I'm not really their granddaughter, and I think they only put up with me on account of Leonard. After he left, they even started giving Mama the cold shoulder."

"Why?"

"Because she had me without being married."

"So who appointed them judge and jury?"

I shrugged.

"Maybe they're the ones who drove her to drink."

"No, I can't blame them for that," I said sadly. "Mama started drinking when her folks died in the fire. I don't know for sure, but I'd almost bet she drank when I came along, too. She had to take care of me by herself for four years, until she met Leonard."

"And he turned out to be a loser."

"Not always. There were good times. In fact, it

wasn't until after he left that I started seriously thinking about my real dad. Who he is, where he is, what
he looks like."

"Bummer," said Alice.

I was staring at a Barbie doll and thinking about
Tina's fit at the fairgrounds when Alice startled me by
slapping the tabletop and yelling, "Birth certificate!"
I banged my knee on the table, and needles of pain
shot down my leg.

"I bet your birth certificate tells who your father
is," she said. "You've got one someplace, or you'd
never have been allowed in kindergarten."

I shot out of the chair. "Alice Murdock, you're a
genius."

She blew on her fingernails and polished them on
her shirt. "I know," she said. "I'm a real cracker-
jack."

✦

I scritched as quietly as a mouse, so Effie wouldn't
hear me as I searched Mama's room for my birth
certificate. Feeling like a snoop, especially because
Mama was flat on her back in the hospital, I sorted
through boxes filled with old receipts, love letters
from Leonard, income tax papers, and artwork I'd
done in kindergarten and first grade.

I ran across one birth certificate—Jackie's. Attached to it was a yellowed clipping from *The Kansas
City Star*, announcing his arrival into the world. Jackson Ramsdale had weighed six pounds, ten ounces,
and had measured nineteen inches long.

I'd been born in Kansas City, too, but there wasn't one smidgen of information relating to that. Had Mama destroyed the evidence to keep me from learning the identity of my father? Why? If he was so bad, what had attracted her to him in the first place?

The *Star* clipping gave me an idea. Since newspapers recorded history as it happened, an old issue of *The Gabriel Gazette* would tell about the fire that had killed Mama's folks. I put back the boxes and hurried to the library.

Mr. Finley was inspecting a damaged book with Mrs. Plummer, who manned the checkout desk. Next to her silvery blue hair and heavy rouge, his head looked pale as a crystal ball. When he saw me, he said, "Well, here's our spelling champ. Boys been breaking your door down since they saw your picture in the paper?"

"Not exactly."

He winked at me and pretended to smooth back a lock of hair. "I had to remind Mrs. Plummer here that I'm a married man."

"Rufus Finley! That's not so!"

Finger on lips, he said, "Quiet, please. You're in the library."

Normally, I would have enjoyed his teasing, but today I was on a mission. "Mr. Friendly," I said, "I need to look up an old edition of *The Gazette*."

"How old?"

"Fourteen years."

"Do you know the month?" he asked as we walked to the room where the microfilm reader and documents were stored.

I scrunched my forehead, recalling the date on my grandparents' tombstones. "May, I think. Sometime in May."

Mr. Finley checked the labels on a file cabinet. "Ah, here we go." He took a metal cannister from a drawer, threaded its film into the reading machine, and showed me how to advance the film by hand. "Give me a holler if you need any help," he said, and left me to dig up the past by myself.

With a whole month of papers to read, I knew I'd be here all night unless I developed a system. Starting with May first, I scanned the daily obituary pages, looking for the names of the Averys. When I found the right one, on May twenty-seventh, I turned back to the day before and read this story on the front page:

Gabriel was struck by tragedy Friday night when a blast caused by a gas leak killed four members of the Charles Avery family in their home at 318 Mimosa Drive.

When firemen arrived on the scene at 12:54 A.M., they found the dwelling engulfed in flames. They were unable to rescue Avery, 38; his wife Marie, 37; and their two children, Thomas Jackson, 15, and Josie Ann, 13.

Witnesses said the Averys' older daughter, Mary Margaret, 18, arrived home with friends while the fire was still blazing. When a reporter tried to talk to her, he was struck by one of her companions. The reporter, Adam Becker, was treated at the hospital for a broken nose. His alleged assailant was not identified.

Due to the possibility of other gas leaks, about

a dozen families were evacuated to the high
school overnight. This morning, Mayor Edward
Watts called for the utility company to make an
all-out inspection of gas lines, to prevent such a
tragedy from happening again. . . .

An overwhelming sadness swept over me. Mama's
whole family had been wiped out, and all she had to
show for it was a few paragraphs in the newspaper.
For a long time, I sat staring at the screen, wondering
about the friend who'd slugged the reporter. I pictured him as Mama's knight in shining armor. Could
he have been my father? And if so, why had she
wanted to erase him from her past?

✦

That evening, Effie called the hospital's third-floor
nurses' station to check on Mama. When she hung up
the phone, Jackie and I were standing by, anxiously
awaiting the verdict.

"You can wipe the gloom off your faces," she said.
"The nurse said Mary Margaret ate some supper and
took a little walk down the hall. Sounds like she slept
off the sickness. Now, who wants to sit with me on the
porch?"

We went outside, but not before Jackie'd found his
race car, Effie'd picked up her quilting, and I'd
grabbed my book.

"Ahhh," said Effie, drawing her lungs full of air as
she lowered herself onto the swing. "Compared to
this afternoon, this feels almost cool."

I sat beside her, and Jackie started running his car around the porch rail. I watched my little brother, who was sometimes purring, sometimes vooming, and vowed that if the agency tried to separate us, they'd have a fight on their hands.

Soon the creaking and clanking of the chain on the swing relaxed me enough to read. I opened my book and lost myself in the Civil War.

8
RAILROADED

The next morning, I called the nurses' station, and a woman told me to hang on a minute and talk to Mama myself. After a couple of buzzes and a blip, she said, "Hello?"

"Hi, Mama. How are you?"

"I'm antsy. I want out of here."

"When are you coming home?"

"After I've seen the doctor and he signs a release."

She didn't sound upset, so I figured she didn't know yet that Doctor Rhiner was going to refer her to a counselor, and that Miss Harbaugh was wanting to send her to a treatment center. "You want me to come over and walk home with you?"

"No, it's too blamed hot. I'll catch a ride with somebody."

"OK. Jackie and Effie say 'hi.' And Mama, I—"

"Yes, Freedom?"

I wanted to tell her I loved her, but the words wouldn't come. I was afraid she wouldn't say she loved me back. "Nothing. We'll be looking for you after a while."

✦

I was reading on the porch when Miss Harbaugh brought Mama home around twelve-thirty.

Mama jumped out of the car and slammed the door, and it was obvious that she was mad. The temperature seemed to shoot up about ten degrees. I knew in an instant that she wasn't going to any alcohol treatment center if she had anything to say about it.

"Two o'clock," called Miss Harbaugh before driving away.

Mama muttered something under her breath and stomped right past me into the house. She was wearing the checkered sundress, but her hair was clean and shiny and pulled back neatly in a pony tail.

I followed her inside and asked, "What's the matter?"

"Blamed meddlers, that's what they are," she said, rubbing her arms as she paced the living room. "Doctor Rhiner suggested I see a counselor. A *shrink!* That was bad enough, but then Miss Harbaugh stuck her nose into it and said I should be put away for a while. Just who do they think they're dealing with here? Mr. Potato Head? This is the United States of America, and they can't be telling me what to do!"

I felt giddy with relief. I couldn't help it. I knew it would be the best thing all around if Mama would get help drying out, but still, I was relieved. We could go on like we had before. No extra strain for Effie, no juvenile justice center, no foster home. Just Mama and Jackie and me. All I had to do was make things easier for her, so she wouldn't have to drink.

She went to the kitchen, yanked on the faucet, and sloshed cold water on her face. When she reached into the drawer for a dish towel, I was glad I'd done the laundry the day before.

"Want me to make some iced tea?" I asked.

"No, thanks," Mama said, opening the cabinet under the sink. "What I need is a little nip."

How could she possibly want a drink after all she'd been through and put *us* through? I was so disgusted, I forgot my promise to please her. Narrowing my eyes, I said, "It's not there. You took it to your bedroom, remember?"

Mama started toward her room, and I said, "It's not there, either."

She whirled around, her eyes wild. "You didn't pour it out?"

"I put it in a safe place."

"So get it."

I gripped the edge of the table to keep my hands from shaking. "If I do, are you going to get falling-down drunk again? Maybe die the next time? Mama, Miss Harbaugh was here yesterday. She told us you can't afford to keep drinking."

She snorted. "What does Miss Harbaugh know about anything? She's never had a husband or children, and she's probably never had a drink stronger than a cream soda."

"She knows the laws in this state. She knows she can take Jackie and me away from you. She's tired of investigating us for the same old garbage." I was about to cry, but I had to get this off my chest. My voice quivered as I pleaded, "Mama, don't you realize what's at stake here? It's not just your life you're gambling with. It's Jackie's and mine, too. Just one more incident like we had the other night, and we'll be out of this house. Is that what you want?"

"No, no, no," she moaned, sinking into a chair and holding her head in her hands. "It's just that I haven't had a drink in over twenty-four hours, and I *need* one, bad!"

"One drink?" I said raggedly. "Since when have you settled for just one drink?"

"Just one. Just one little nip. Miss Harbaugh is going with me this afternoon to talk to my boss about my—going away."

"But you said—"

"I was just letting off steam. I'm caught between a rock and a hard place. If I go for treatment, she'll find you kids a temporary home. If I don't, she'll seek legal custody and take you anyway."

My bubble of hope deflated. Jackie and I were goners. Move over, Patsy McCorkle, here we come.

"So you see why I need that nip. Without it, I can't do it. Can't face the boss, can't face the stares and speculation."

Every ounce of energy had drained out of me, and I didn't have the strength to fight. I went to the cupboard for a glass, then into my room and poured Mama a shot of whiskey.

✦

Effie dolloped a spoonful of chicken and dumplings onto Jackie's plate and passed the bowl to me. My appetite had sailed out the window the minute Miss Harbaugh brought Mama back from the factory with a stack of papers to fill out, but I served myself a dumpling so I could chase it around on my plate.

"So it's all settled?" asked Effie.

"It looks that way," sighed Mama.

I knew she was skeptical about the treatment center. So was I. How could fourteen years of drinking be resolved in thirty days?

"Mr. Carpenter said I could take a leave of absence and still have a job when I get back."

"But he won't pay you for not working," I said. "What'll we do about the rent?"

Mama's fingers toyed nervously with the buttons on her shirt. "Miss Harbaugh said she could get us some government assistance."

"Assistance?" I squeaked. "You mean charity? You always said Averys don't take charity. We'll use my savings, and I'll get more baby-sitting jobs."

"I won't take money from my kids."

"But you'll take a handout from the government," I said, incredulous.

"Now just hold on here, Freedom," said Effie. "Don't think of it as a handout. Think of it as a bonus for all the years Mary Margaret has paid income tax."

Effie's eyes were pleading with me not to make it harder for Mama than it already was. I swallowed with difficulty and glanced down at my plate. The dumpling looked like a glob of wallpaper paste, and I laid my napkin over it.

"So," Effie said brightly, "when do you go?"

"Monday. Miss Harbaugh's driving me to the city."

"And the kids can stay here?"

"No, that's the worst part. Miss Harbaugh's going to find someplace else for them to stay. Because of your age and your heart."

"Well, I can't do a thing about my age, but my heart's OK now. It's like that commercial on TV. It takes a licking and keeps on ticking."

"You know that, and I know it, but Miss Harbaugh's supervisor said no."

My eyes met Jackie's across the table. He looked like he'd just swallowed a frog.

"I want to stay with Effie," he said.

Effie reached over and patted his arm. "It'll be all right, hon. You'll see. Miss Harbaugh'll do her best for you."

I knew I'd throw a tantrum if I heard Miss Harbaugh's name one more time. I raked my chair away from the table and stood up. "May I be excused?"

"What's your hurry? You haven't eaten," said Effie, eyeing the telltale lump the napkin was hiding on my plate.

"This is Friday, and I've got to baby-sit. I want to take a bath and wash my hair before I go."

"Well, all right," Effie said, "but grab a handful of cookies to snack on. And when you get there, lock the doors and check all the windows. You never know when some maniac'll be on the loose."

Later, as I left our bathroom, I was startled by Mama standing in the hall. In her hand was the whiskey she'd found hidden in the return-air vent in my room. Turnabout is fair play, I thought. I snooped in Mama's room, and she snooped in mine.

"Don't say a word," she said. "I've got to have a little nip, or I won't sleep a wink."

✦

Since Bonnie's singing job didn't end until the wee hours, I stayed the night at her house, as usual. Saturday morning, I slipped quietly in our back door. The aroma of coffee filled the kitchen. I loved the smell of coffee, but I didn't much care for the taste, so I poured myself only half a cup and went looking for Mama. Maybe if she saw me acting like a grown-up, she'd treat me like one.

I'd thought about it most of the night. I was a teenager now—old enough to be responsible for Jackie and me. We could stay here by ourselves while Mama was gone. All we needed was for her to convince Miss Harbaugh that we'd be fine, because Effie would be next door.

I found Mama on the couch in the living room, reading the morning's mail. "Hi," I said. "Anything for me?"

With a start, she folded a letter and slid it into its envelope, which she hid under the rest of the mail in her hand. "Nothing but bills," she said calmly, but her face was as white as the paper she'd stashed away, and her deep blue eyes were troubled. "How were Bonnie's boys?"

"Little angels," I said as I sat beside her. "I read them to sleep about nine o'clock, and they didn't even turn over all night."

"That's good." Mama wrapped the tie of her raggedy bathrobe around her finger, then unwound it and wrapped it again.

"Only two maniacs tried to break in," I said, hoping to coax a smile out of her.

"Since when did you start drinking coffee? It'll stunt your growth."

"Mama, it can't stunt my growth. I'm already half a head taller than you and still growing." I laughed and added, "Effie tells me coffee'll turn my feet black. You two act like I'm still a little kid. I'm thirteen now."

"And trying to act thirty."

"No, I'm not. I'm just trying to make you see that I'm old enough to take care of things around here while you're gone."

"No way," said Mama, and her eyes darted nervously toward the mail.

"Mama, what's the matter? Who's that letter from?"

"Freedom Avery, you're getting as bad as Hilda Harbaugh, always meddling in my private business." She got up and yanked at the tie of her robe to tighten it, then stalked off down the hall, taking the mail along with her.

I stared after her, seething that I was old enough to do the laundry, shopping, cooking, and housework, but too young to be told about one measly letter.

I marched into the kitchen and dumped my coffee into the sink with a splat. On impulse, I opened the cabinet underneath. The whiskey bottle wasn't there.

✦

Before the day was over, I was wondering if there was a place in the *Guinness Book of World Records* for the longest little nip in history. Mama polished off her bottle and walked to the bank to cash her paycheck so she could buy another.

She came home carrying a brown sack from the liquor store and a white one from the bakery. "Mr. Solomon swears I'm trying to fatten you up," she said, removing two great gooey cinnamon rolls from the bakery bag.

"Thanks, Mama," I said. It was her payday ritual: cheap whiskey for her, day-old rolls for Jackie and me.

I watched as she smeared margarine on the rolls, popped them in the oven, and poured herself a drink. Soon the aroma of hot cinnamon and icing replaced the scent of whiskey.

Jackie came flying in the back door, declaring, "I smell cinnamon rolls."

"Jackie Ramsdale, have you got radar?" asked Mama.

"Nope, just a good smeller."

We laughed, and Jackie and I devoured the rolls and licked the last sugary bits from our fingers.

Mama drained her glass and leaned over to wipe icing off Jackie's mouth. Cradling his chin in her hand, she gazed into his eyes. "I won't be around to buy goodies next week," she said wistfully.

That was Mama—singling out one little detail and missing the big picture altogether. Next week she'd be undergoing treatment, and Jackie and I'd be at the mercy of strangers, and here she was getting bummed out about cinnamon rolls. It was like worrying about dust on the furniture before the earthquake hit.

✦

I baby-sat again that night, then went with Jackie to Sunday school the next morning. We spent a pleasant afternoon, playing rummy with Mama, who was cheerfully tipsy. After supper, I helped Mama pack her suitcase, and talked her into washing her hair so I could curl it.

I fetched her box of plastic rollers and carried it to the kitchen. Still wearing the towel on her head, she was pouring more whiskey into a smudgy glass. At my look of disapproval, she said, "No lectures, hon. Starting tomorrow, this stuff will be just a memory."

She sat down at the table, and I removed the towel and combed the tangles from her hair. As I sectioned off a honey-colored strand to wind it around a roller, I said, "We need a blow dryer and a curling iron. Then you wouldn't have to sleep on bristles."

"We need other things worse, like a new clutch for the truck."

"But I'd pay for the dryer and curling iron."

"That would be just the beginning. Next you'd

want lipstick and eye shadow, and you're not old enough yet."

"Other girls my age wear makeup."

"Not Alice. She didn't have any goop on her face at the fairgrounds."

"She's a writer. She's different. And she doesn't have freckles and a honker like mine."

"Your nose isn't that big, and makeup wouldn't hide it, if it was."

"But Mama—"

"Be a kid while you can. When people grow up too fast, they make bad decisions, and then they have to live with their mistakes."

And wasn't I walking proof of that? I wanted to ask Mama about my birth certificate then, but I kept quiet. I knew she wouldn't tell me anyway, and we'd end up in a big fight on her last night at home.

✦

I didn't sleep very well, and every time I woke up, I heard Mama walking the floor. At six-thirty in the morning, I rolled Jackie out of bed, so we could spend a little time with her before Miss Harbaugh came.

Mama was already dressed, and she looked unhealthy in a peach-colored blouse and a pair of navy slacks that billowed around her skinny hips. Her eyes were bright, her hands shaky. I glanced at the counter—at the coffee pot almost empty and the whiskey bottle more than half full.

While Jackie and I were eating breakfast, Mama asked, "What kind of cereal is that?"

"Cheerios," I said.

"You could have fooled me. From the looks on your faces, I thought it was Gloomios."

I smiled at her. She was being brave, and I loved her fiercely for it. My emotions were all in a jumble. I was sad that she was leaving. Frustrated that she had to go. Angry that she'd been railroaded by Hilda Harbaugh. Afraid of what the future would bring for all of us.

A few minutes before eight, Effie came over to see Mama off. Motioning to the bottle, she said, "Mary Margaret, don't you think it's time to get rid of that?"

"Abble-solutely," Mama said, and made a big production of pouring it down the sink.

When Miss Harbaugh knocked on the door, Effie said, "You all say your good-byes in private. I'll let her in."

While Mama was telling Jackie to be good, I caught part of the conversation in the living room.

". . . drinking all weekend," Effie said.

". . . for thirty days just to get their kids back, and they don't really intend to change."

Mama touched my arm. "Freedom," she said, "I'll miss you."

"I'll miss you, too." I stepped into her arms, bumping my chin on her forehead. She smelled of clean hair and laundry soap and just a hint of whiskey, and having her arms around me felt awkward and comforting at the same time. I squeezed her hard.

Jackie's face was as white as his hair, and I could see he was about to cry. I took his hand, and Mama took the other, and we walked reluctantly into the living room.

Effie and Miss Harbaugh were watching us with sympathetic eyes. The social worker said, "I know it's hard, but just tell yourselves that this is all for the best. Are you ready?"

Mama sniffed and nodded.

I looked to see if she was crying, but she kept her face down, and I couldn't tell if her eyes were wet. "Mama," I said softly, "I'll write to you. Will you write back?"

"I'm sorry," said Miss Harbaugh, "but the rules are that your mother can have no outside contact for two weeks. The idea is for her to start off with a clean slate and concentrate on getting well, not on what's going on at home. When the two weeks are up, she'll be able to send mail and receive it and even make telephone calls. . . . Oh, Mrs. Ramsdale, I almost forgot, you'll have to leave your watch here. They won't let you keep valuables at the center."

Mama slipped the watch from her wrist and handed it to me. "Wear it for good luck until I get back," she said, and I heard tears in her voice.

My stomach hurt and my throat ached, and I thought if this went on much longer, I'd start blubbering, and I was too tough to cry in front of Miss Harbaugh.

"OK, then, let's go," Miss Harbaugh said. "You children mind Mrs. Waisner today and help her all you can. I'll be back tomorrow, and we'll work out a different arrangement."

An arrangement. As if Jackie and I were lilies at a flower show. Suddenly, I no longer wanted to cry, but to throw something.

Effie hugged Mama. "Now don't you worry about a thing," she said. "Just get yourself straightened out. Get rid of those demons from the past, so you and these young'uns can have a better future."

Mama nodded. She bent to pick up the suitcase I'd set by the door, but Jackie grabbed it and said, "I'll carry it."

I watched him struggle outside with it, followed by Mama, the social worker, and Effie. I stayed in the house, just so Miss Harbaugh would know she didn't have my blessing for splitting up our family.

9

THE PLAN

 "Let's bake some chocolate chip cookies," said Effie.

"Hey, yeah," replied Jackie.

I loved Effie dearly, but her solution for every problem was to whip up something with chocolate. It was a wonder she hadn't put chocolate in the dumplings last night. That nasty thought made the Cheerios sit like ball bearings in my stomach. "Not me," I said. I wanted to sit and stare at the wall and feel sorry for myself, but Effie wasn't having any of that.

"Freedom Avery, you march yourself out that door and into my kitchen this minute. You're not going to lie around and mope."

I marched.

Effie supervised and told stories while Jackie and I measured and poured and stirred. Even though I was a captive audience, I got caught up in her tales.

"When I was a girl, we didn't have to worry about social workers down in the Ozarks," she chuckled. "Town folks stayed away from Copperhead Holler, 'cause of the timber rattlers, cottonmouths, and copperheads. The bite of a timber rattler could kill a man, and a cottonmouth or copperhead could make him plenty sick."

"Why would anybody live in a snaky place like that?" I asked.

"You don't know different if you've never lived different. You just grow up watching where you step. And staying in the house after dark, 'cause that's when the copperheads come out."

"Did you ever get bit?" asked Jackie.

"Pert' near. One day, when I lifted the washtub, there was a big old copperhead stretched out underneath it, not two inches from my bare feet. I dropped the tub and went running for the axe and chopped that snake in half." Effie's creaky old body shuddered. "That was fifty-eight years ago, but I never forgot the smell."

"The smell?" I said.

"A copperhead's got a musty odor, like wet moss or rotten bark. It's nature's warning, same as a rattlesnake shaking its tail."

All this talk of snakes was giving me the willies, but Effie was just getting wound up.

"One other time, I had a close call," she said. "Didn't get home soon enough and found myself walking through the woods at dusk. I caught a whiff of a copperhead, and I jumped two feet high. The snake struck a tree instead of me. The tree died."

That seemed pretty farfetched to me, but Jackie believed it. I could have scraped his eyeballs off with a spoon handle.

Effie's eyes twinkled as she went on spinning her yarn. "The Ozarks is famous for two things—water and snakes. When they flooded that land down south to make Truman Lake, rattlesnakes swarmed out by the thousands and got squashed on the highways and shot by farmers. Later, I heard a rumor that the conservation department was restocking rattlesnakes—taking them up in helicopters and dropping them from the air."

Before I knew it, the cookies were baked and Effie was digging in her refrigerator to see what to serve for lunch. I volunteered to get some hot dogs from home. Effie lived on a fixed income, and money was as tight for her as it was for us.

I left her warm kitchen and went into ours, which felt as gloomy as a tomb with Mama gone. There was her cracked coffee cup on the counter, still half full of black liquid, and there were our cereal bowls on the table. The clock on the wall ticked loudly, counting off the hours until Miss Harbaugh would come to haul Jackie and me away.

While picking up the bowls, I discovered a cockroach feasting on a Cheerio that was stuck to the table. I whacked him with the flyswatter, then scraped him into the trash.

Disposable, I thought. That's what Jackie and I are to Hilda Harbaugh.

✦

After lunch, Effie curled up on the couch to watch her soaps, and Jackie wandered outside to find Mike. I fidgeted around the house and finally hustled out the door and up the street. I felt lost, wrung out, and helpless. I thought about going to the library, but I wasn't up to Mr. Friendly's good humor. I thought about going to Alice's house, until I remembered it was Monday, the day her family visited her grandparents in Pink Eye.

Driven to go *somewhere,* to do *something,* I hurried on aimlessly, across the railroad tracks and up Hackberry Street. Heat waves rose from the sidewalk, and I could feel the freckles almost melting off my face. Still, I continued on.

I swept on past the junk store and ended up in the park. In the singeing heat of early afternoon, it was deserted, except for a young man who was reading *Goldilocks and the Three Bears* to two little girls on a shaded bench. He was trying to make a squeaky voice for Baby Bear and a growly voice for Papa Bear, but he kept getting mixed up. The girls squealed with laughter, and the bigger one said, "Oh, Daddy, Baby Bear doesn't growl."

"Yes, he does," said her father, " 'cause he's got a frog in his throat."

A-plus for ingenuity, I thought, and gave the man a nine.

Sometimes I'd go for days, not thinking about my father. But other times, like now, I was hounded with jealousy. It wasn't fair. I'd missed out on having a father read to me, look out for me, love me.

I sat on the merry-go-round and scuffed my feet on the ground to start myself spinning slowly. After a few rounds, when dizziness set in, I let myself go limp and my mind wander. Closing my eyes, I imagined I was bobbing along peacefully in a boat. Leonard had rented boats when we went camping and . . . My eyes popped open as an idea struck like lightning.

Truman Lake.

Jackie and I would run away! And camp out at the lake!

I dragged my feet to stop the merry-go-round, but my mind continued spinning as I laid out a plan. There was some food at home, and the tent Leonard had bought for Jackie and me, and I had my savings account. After Effie was in bed, we'd leave tonight, on foot, but we'd throw Miss Harbaugh off our trail by making her think we'd ridden the Amtrak to St. Louis.

My spirits were high as I hopped off the merry-go-round and headed home. That snoopy old social worker wouldn't get her hands on Jackie and me. When she showed up tomorrow with her briefcase and an armload of papers, she'd discover that my little brother and I had flown the coop.

At Effie's house, I eased in the back door and peeked into the living room. She was sleeping on the couch. After looking up Amtrak in the phone book, I dialed the toll-free number.

"Thank you for calling Amtrak. How may I help you?"

"How much for two tickets from Gabriel, Missouri, to St. Louis?"

"It's thirty-three dollars one way for adults and half

fare for children. The next train leaves at 10:42 P.M., arriving at St. Louis at 2:15 A.M."

"Hold on," I said, "I'm writing this down." Of course, I didn't need to know the exact times, except that I wanted enough information to convince Miss Harbaugh we'd left on the train.

"Reservations are not required. Since there is no ticket office in Gabriel, you may buy your tickets on board or from a travel agent."

"Thank you," I said and replaced the receiver quietly.

I slipped out the back way, went next door, and found my passbook. Counting my savings, and the ten dollars Bonnie had paid me for Friday and Saturday, I had one hundred thirty-one dollars.

I made a list of all the things we'd need—tent, sleeping bags, food, utensils, can opener, clothes, toiletries, books, map, squirt bottle filled with vinegar. The last item was in case we got chased by a dog, and I considered it a stroke of pure genius that I'd thought of it.

I reread the list, then composed a note to leave for Effie. Being careful not to lie or to give away any clues, I wrote:

> Dear Effie,
>   I'm sorry to leave without saying good-bye. You're terrific—better than a grandmother.
>   Since you hate the idea of living in a rest home, I know you'll understand why we have to go. Jackie and I would be just as miserable

*in a foster home. Remember what you told us
about the whipping post, that no person
should ever lay claim against another? That's
the way I feel about Miss Harbaugh.*

*Please tell Bonnie I won't be able to baby-sit
for a while, but that Alice Murdock would be
good with the boys.*

*Don't worry about us. We have money and
we'll be fine. Thanks for everything.*

Love, Freedom

As I put the note aside with the Amtrak information,
I felt a twinge of guilt. Effie *would* worry. There was
no doubt about that.

I found the Missouri map and discovered that Truman Lake was about thirty-five miles due south of
Gabriel on Highway 65. We'd have to take the back
roads, of course, but maybe they'd run fairly parallel
to the highway.

Next, I began gathering up the items on the list and
packing them in the laundry basket. In the bedroom,
my spelling trophy dazzled in a beam of sunlight, as
if reminding me that it should be engraved. "Later,"
I muttered as I pulled the newspaper clipping out from
under it and stuck it in my pocket.

I glanced longingly at the books I'd bought from
Second Time Around, wishing I could take them all.
After choosing two for me and two for Jackie, I went
into the kitchen.

The foods that wouldn't spoil—cereal, crackers,

cookies, bread, and potatoes—went onto the pile, along with lard, matches, and salt.

I looked in the deep freeze to check the ice. Two jugs would provide us with cold water for a few days. If we ran out, surely we'd be able to fill up someplace.

When I'd packed everything, I stashed the basket in Mama's closet. It weighed a ton, but I couldn't think of one item that we could do without. How in the world would I lug it for thirty-five miles?

Then I remembered the wagon Jackie had wanted at the junk store. Henry was asking twenty dollars for it, but he always jacked up the price. I figured I could get it for fifteen, easy, if he hadn't already sold it.

I walked to the bank and withdrew my savings. Keeping out a twenty for the wagon, I stuffed the rest in my pocket and headed for the junk store across the street.

Henry was showing some bunk beds to a woman with two rowdy little boys. The boys were climbing up and down the ladder, jumping on the mattresses, and arguing over who was going to sleep on top. I coughed at the smell of dust and old urine they'd stirred up, but I was glad to have a chance to look at the wagon without Henry breathing down my neck.

Trying to appear nonchalant, I moseyed over to the used toys. The wagon was still there. I untangled it from the mess of cars and tricycles so I could examine it.

Its bed was about a foot and a half wide and more than three feet long. Someone had painted it bright red, although I could see little bumps of rust beneath the paint. The tongue seemed strong and the wheels in good shape, but I pulled it down the aisle to make sure. It rolled easily on the wooden floor, despite one squeaky wheel.

"Wagon, wagon, pants are draggin'," chirped one of the little boys. "Can I have a ride?"

Henry and the woman were looking at me curiously. "What a nice wagon," she said. "How much is it?"

I tightened my grip on the handle as Henry replied, "Twenty dollars. They go for about sixty new."

"Can we get it, Mommy?" asked the boy, climbing in.

"I'm buying it," I said stiffly.

The boy crawled out and started bawling, and Henry grinned at me. For once, I hadn't been able to con him into a lower price.

I plunked the twenty-dollar bill on the counter and wheeled the wagon out the door. As it rattled behind me down the sidewalk, I told myself that the five dollars I'd lost on the deal was a bargain if it meant freedom. Freedom for Freedom, the squeaky wheel seemed to say.

Before long, I realized the squeak presented a problem. Effie was bound to hear it and wonder why I'd suddenly gotten the urge to buy a wagon. I'd have to hide it someplace.

As I crossed the railroad tracks, I came up with a solution. The depot wasn't used much anymore, and the storage shed behind it was unlocked, a fact I'd discovered one day while searching for Mike and Jackie.

I went to the shed, looked around to see that no one was watching, and stashed the wagon inside.

By Mama's watch, it was almost five o'clock. Only six hours till blast-off.

10

THE GETAWAY

After supper, Jackie talked Effie and me into playing rummy. Usually, I was good at it, but tonight I couldn't concentrate. In less than two hours, we'd be sneaking out into the darkness and heading for Truman Lake.

"Freedom, you can't pick up that nine and not play it," Jackie said.

"What? Oh, sorry." I put the nine back on the discard pile, then drew and discarded a seven.

He pounced on it, laid out four sevens, and discarded a queen. "Rummy!" he crowed.

I grinned at him absentmindedly and made a mental note to take his cards when we left.

"Minus sixty," said Effie, yawning as she tallied up her score. "I've been tromped enough for one night."

"Just one more hand," pleaded Jackie.

Effie glanced at the clock. "Well, all right," she said, "but these eyes close in fifteen minutes."

I smiled at her. She was so predictable. She'd be conked out by ten o'clock, but she'd be up with the sun in the morning. If Jackie and I left at eleven, we'd have no more than a seven-hour head start before Effie discovered we were gone.

✦

We all went to bed before ten. Jackie took the couch, while I lay on a quilt spread out on the floor, my heart clattering to the rhythm of the fan.

When I was sure Effie and Jackie were asleep, I retrieved the cookset from where I'd hidden it under the couch and slipped out the back door, letting go a little squeak when I stubbed my toe in the dark.

A flashlight. How could I have forgotten a flashlight? I'd have to dig for one in Mama's closet.

Our kitchen looked spooky from the glow of the street light in the alley. The only sounds were the rumbling of the freezer on the back porch and the wall clock ticking, "Run away! Run away!" I felt my way down the hall to Mama's bedroom and into the closet, where I closed the door before pulling the string for the light. Two cockroaches skittered up the wall, and I frowned, hoping none had invaded our basket.

On a shelf beside the flashlight was Mama's senior yearbook. I picked it up and thumbed through it until I saw her face smiling up at me. I smiled a sad smile back at her, then closed the book and stuck it in the laundry basket.

After hauling the basket to the kitchen, I changed from my nightgown into a pair of cutoffs and a T-shirt. Standing still for a moment, I checked things off in my mind. All set. I slipped out of our house and into Effie's kitchen, where I left the note and the

Amtrak information on the table before going in to wake Jackie.

Effie was snoring so loudly I could hear her from the living room, but I walked on tiptoes to the couch. "Jackie," I whispered, "wake up."

He moaned and rolled over.

"Wake up. It's important."

"Wait a minute. I've got to get this boat out of the water."

I grinned. Jackie dreamed in 3-D, and I'd seen him get out of bed and turn somersaults, sound asleep. "I'll help you," I said. "You go around to the other side and pull. I'll push."

Jackie got up and started pulling at the couch. Now that I had him up and moving, I grabbed his sneakers and led him out the back door.

"Freedom," he said, finally waking up, "what's going on?"

"Shhh, be quiet or you'll wake Effie. We're leaving."

He looked around at the blackness of the night and said, "Leaving? It's dark out here."

"I know. We can go and not get caught."

"Caught? Who's after us?" he asked fearfully.

"Nobody yet, but we're running away from Miss Harbaugh."

"Ohhhh," he breathed, beginning to understand. "Where are we running to?"

"I'll tell you later," I said as I steered him toward our back door. "Come and change clothes and put your shoes on. We've got to hightail it out of here."

When Jackie was dressed, I gave him two jugs of ice to carry and picked up the bulging laundry basket. We left our house without looking back.

By the time we'd covered the three blocks to the depot, Jackie's fingers were nearly frozen and my arms felt paralyzed. I set the basket down on the ground so I could roll the wagon out of the shed.

"You bought the wagon?" Jackie asked softly, pulling it over to look at it under a streetlight.

"Yes, thank goodness," I said as I massaged my arms. When the feeling came back, I lifted the basket and the ice jugs into the wagon. "Come on. We've got a long ways to go. No more talking for a while."

We headed south on Birch Street, moving quietly as ghosts, except for the faint squeak of the wheel. A few dogs barked, but none came chasing after us.

When we passed Alice's house, I saw a light in her bedroom window and knew she was reading *The Count of Monte Cristo*. I wanted to stop and tell her we were leaving, but I couldn't. If she didn't know our destination, nobody could pry it out of her.

Eventually, houses and streetlights became scarce, and the blacktop road ran into gravel. Only then did I feel it was safe to talk. "Remember the times we camped out at Truman Lake?" I asked.

"Is that where we're going?"

"Yes."

"I don't remember very much. Tell me," said Jackie, who'd been only five when his dad left.

"Leonard always chose a campsite close to the water. You and I'd wade in the shallows, while he and

Mama fished. One time she hooked a nine-pound catfish that almost pulled her into the lake."

Jackie giggled. "I bet she thought she was catching a whale."

"Those were good times. It's too bad—" I stopped myself. No sense tormenting ourselves with old memories.

"Freedom, what's wrong with us?"

"Wrong? Nothing's wrong."

"Then why did Daddy leave, and why is Mama always drinking?"

"I don't know, but it's not because there's something wrong with us," I said firmly. I'd read somewhere that children of alcoholics suffer from low self-esteem, and I wasn't going to let that happen to my little brother.

"Will Mama be different when she gets home?"

"She'll be healthy and pretty as a picture, and she won't have to have her little nips to think straight." But is that true? I wondered. Miss Harbaugh had told Effie some people went away just to get their kids back. Did that mean the treatment might not work? Would Mama come home and pick up her drinking where she'd left off?

"When Mama quits drinking, maybe Daddy'll come back," Jackie said.

"Don't count on that. He likes Idaho."

"I know. Freedom, why don't you have a dad?"

"Everybody's got a dad. Mine just didn't marry Mama."

"Who is he?"

"I don't know. And stop asking so many questions." On that lonely road in the darkness, the hole in my soul was a chasm.

We walked on silently, slapping at mosquitoes and listening to the night sounds. Katydids chirped, an owl hooted, and frogs chug-a-rummed in a pond. Occasionally, we heard truck traffic over on Highway 65. Those comforting noises made me determined to go on all night, to put as many miles as possible between us and Miss Harbaugh.

When yard lights in the distance showed us the way, I switched off the flashlight to save the batteries. Once, at the sound of faraway howling, I dug out the vinegar bottle and Jackie stuffed a handful of rocks into his shorts pocket.

"Uh-oh," I said, when I saw headlights approaching. "We'd better hide." We dragged the wagon into a ditch and crouched down behind some weeds that I knew would be loaded with chiggers. Bug bites I could handle. What worried me was stepping on a snake or a varmint.

While we waited for the vehicle, I puffed air like a locomotive, sniffing for copperheads. Finally, a pickup roared past, and we heard drunken voices and heavy metal music. A can came flying out the window and grazed my face.

"P.U.," I said as a few drops of beer dribbled under my nose. Alice was right. It did smell like it belonged in a horse.

"Hey, Freed," said Jackie, reaching for the can, "why don't we gather up all the cans we see? Make people think we're just out picking up litter instead of running away."

I stared at him in astonishment. "For eight years old, you've sure got a criminal mind. From now on, you'll be the brains of this outfit."

11

ON THE ROAD

"I'm tired," said Jackie—not whining, just making a statement. In the moonlight, his face was pale as uncooked dough.

"Me, too, Cotton Top, but we've got to keep going." I was so tired myself I was cross-eyed, and my hands had blisters from pulling the wagon all night. "When it gets daylight, we'll find a place to rest. Can you hold up for another hour?"

"I can if you can."

I paused long enough to dig out some chocolate chip cookies. "Let's eat these and call it breakfast."

Jackie gave me a halfhearted grin and helped himself to a handful.

We'd been walking the back roads for six hours, stopping only three times to rest and take drinks from the melted ice in a milk jug. I figured if we'd covered a mile every half hour, we were about twelve miles from Gabriel.

Thoughts of Effie haunted me, and I hoped she wouldn't have a heart attack when she got up and discovered we were gone.

The sky grew light, and I said, "Let's start looking for a place to rest. An old barn, some woods—anyplace where we can hole up and sleep for a few hours."

We walked on and on without finding a suitable spot. The barns were all too close to houses, and soybean fields surrounded us. A car popped over a hill and barreled past, leaving us in a cloud of dirt.

At last, we came to a bridge and stopped to stare down into a trickle of water. "Come on," I said. "Let's follow the creek."

It was tough going, pulling the wagon down the hill and over the rocks of the creek bed. Around the bend, we found a sandbar and a little pool of water, shaded by a pair of crooked trees.

"Manna from heaven," I murmured. Jackie and I kicked off our shoes and collapsed onto our sleeping bags. I was asleep before you could say "Hilda Harbaugh."

✦

I awoke with a groan and blinked against the sunlight. My calves were stiff, my blisters hurt, and my ankles were itchy with chigger bites. I checked Mama's watch and saw that it was almost noon. I'd slept for five hours.

There was the wagon, parked in the sun, but Jackie was nowhere in sight. I stretched painfully and yawned. Most of the ice had melted in our milk jugs. I set them in the shade, which was the equivalent of closing the barn door after the cows got out.

The quiet pool beckoned at me, and I waded in

with my clothes on and sat down in the clear, warm water. While the dirt was floating off me, I used a sharp rock to clean my nails. In my mind, I heard Mama calling my fingers "princess pinkies," heard her saying I'd be "Somebody Someday." Didn't she know that I was already somebody? I was *me,* and I wanted to be proud of that. I wanted to know my father. I wanted him to claim me.

Had Mama cried yesterday because she was leaving Jackie, or because she was leaving both of us? Did she really, truly love me, or was I just a mistake, a burden to bear?

I crawled out of the water and sat down on a sun-dappled rock. Miss Harbaugh must be looking for us now. I was sure she'd spend a couple of days trying to track us down in St. Louis before she decided we'd outsmarted her. I wished I had a radio, so I'd know if she'd put out a missing persons bulletin, like we'd often heard in Kansas City.

I was tying my shoes when I heard Jackie coming from farther down the creek. At least, I hoped it was Jackie. I kept my eyes glued to the place he would appear.

He came around the bend, trying to whistle. His hair was slicked down, his clothes damp and fairly clean. "Hi," he said. "I wondered if you were gonna sleep all day."

"How long have you been up?"

"Long enough to wash the chiggers off and see what's down the creek. I'm starved, and I want something besides cookies."

I glanced around the creek bed. "It should be safe

to build a fire. If you'll gather up some dry leaves and firewood, I'll peel some potatoes."

In half an hour, we'd built a fire in a little circle of stones and had the potatoes frying in the skillet from the cookset.

"Mmmm, that looks good," said Jackie when I dished his out.

"Enjoy it. Supper will be cookies and water."

We scarfed down the meal in nothing flat, then spent the afternoon playing rummy and reading. When we got too hot, we waded into the creek with our clothes on, and didn't bother to change when we got out. I'd left our bathing suits at home, because mine was too small and Jackie's had a hole in the seat.

Jackie dozed off after supper, but sleep was out of the question for me. I studied the Missouri map and packed the wagon. About an hour before dark, I woke Jackie. "Come on, little bro. Time to roll."

"Do we have to?"

"Afraid so."

"I wish we had a magic carpet, so we wouldn't have to walk."

"Fat chance. Come on now. Move."

He took his time putting his shoes on, then spent three or four minutes behind a tree where he'd gone to relieve himself.

I sighed. If he was dragging his feet already, the next twenty-three miles would be murder.

❖

We headed south, picking up stray cans and tossing them into the wagon. Three hours later, I was dragging myself along. It was bedtime, and I was exhausted.

Heat lightning flashed in the distance, and Jackie said, "That makes me think of the laser light show at Worlds of Fun."

I smiled at the memory of the amusement park. Mama's boss in the city had given her free tickets, and she'd taken us on Jackie's birthday. "Mama screamed her head off on that big roller coaster," I said.

"The Timber Wolf. You were screaming, too."

"I was not. I was laughing. Well, maybe I did scream a little bit, when the trolley was at the top of that forty-foot drop."

"It wasn't forty feet."

"It sure looked . . . Uh-oh, here comes trouble."

Our voices had alerted a dog at the farmhouse ahead. I almost panicked when I made out its silhouette in the yard light. A Doberman. Huge and snarling and streaking toward us. I grabbed the vinegar bottle. Jackie reached for his rocks.

I wanted to turn tail and run, but I knew if I did that, the dog would tear us to pieces. "Careful, Jackie. Don't make him madder than he already is." The creature came close enough for me to see its teeth. "Easy, boy," I said, heart pounding. "Easy now. We're just passing through."

We kept moving as the Doberman ran circles around us, growling deep in his throat. I wondered if it was true that dogs could smell fear.

"Easy, boy. Easy." I waited until I could have touched him, then squeezed the bottle and gave him a healthy squirt in the face.

The dog yelped, then snorted, spraying me with vinegar and slobbers.

A porch light came on at the house, and a man's voice cut through the night. "Satan, shut up! Get back here and leave that poor rabbit alone!"

Satan retreated with his tail between his legs. I wiped the slime off my hands in the dirt and fought the urge to throw up.

"Whoo-eeee, boy," said the man on the porch. "You stink. What were you chasing? A rabbit, or a dill pickle?"

✦

The batteries in our flashlight gave out sometime after midnight. Jackie and I kept walking, simply because it was too dark to find a place to stop. We stumbled along for a few minutes, feeling our way by the gravel beneath our feet. The odor of skunk added to our misery, and when a whippoorwill called out suddenly, I yelped in fright.

The wagon began to feel like a lead weight, and the blackness seemed to swallow us up. I thought of the time my class visited a cave and the guide turned off all the lights. I'd held my hand directly in front of my face and couldn't even see it. There'd been bats in that cave, clinging to the ceiling like fly specks.

Bats, snakes, spiders, wolves. Who knew what creatures might be lurking ahead, ready to pounce on us?

"Let's sing," I said.

There was no answer.

"Jackie?"

Still no answer. My scalp tingled and I couldn't breathe. Either I'd lost Jackie, or something had grabbed him. I groped around in the darkness until I bumped into something warm and soft. It was Jackie, sitting on top of the cans in the wagon, sound asleep.

That did it. Snakes or monsters or whatever—I couldn't go any farther. After pulling the wagon to the side of the road, I sat down cross-legged, rested my head on Jackie, and dozed off.

When I awoke, the moon was peeking out from behind some smoky-looking clouds, casting an eerie light over a field of hay bales the size of elephants.

"Good enough," I muttered, hauling the wagon over the ditch and behind a bale of hay.

12
THE ENEMY

★ A tractor chugging by on the road woke us up at daylight. We wet a T-shirt to wash our faces, then ate Cheerios straight from the box and drank warm water.

"We'll be traveling in the daytime from now on," I said. "It's too hard in the dark without a flashlight."

"And scary."

I looked at my little brother and wondered, for the first time, if I'd made a mistake taking him away from Gabriel. At least, in a foster home, he'd have hot meals and a bed.

As if reading my mind, he said, "Freed, I'm glad you didn't run away without me."

We left the field and moved on under a sun that showed no mercy. As the temperature climbed, heat waves shimmered off farm machinery and metal barns. My arms prickled with sunburn, and my face felt hot enough to explode. Still, we kept going.

One of the milk jugs was empty, and the other was about a quarter full of hot water. Thirst clogged my throat like a dirty dish rag, and I yearned for a tall Pepsi-Cola glistening with ice.

What if Jackie or I had a heat stroke? Or got sick from sunburn? Or ran out of water and died of thirst? But something kept me going. We were survivors, and we'd get by somehow.

Tar bubbles snapped beneath our feet as we crossed a blacktop road. A sign informed us that Highway 65 was five miles to the west, and the town of Pink Eye was seven miles east. A few yards farther on, I sat in the wagon and found where we were on the map. Truman Lake didn't look far on paper, but I guessed it was still about fifteen miles away.

Soon we were plodding on again. After a while, we came to a two-toned blue pickup parked on the side of the road. Sitting on its tailgate was a five-gallon water cooler.

As my mind registered "ice water," my eyes searched for its owner. When I spotted some men bucking bales in a hayfield, I sidled up to the truck and filled our cups from the spigot. We chugged down the drinks and filled our cups two more times. Never, in all my life, had anything tasted so good.

"Hot, ain't it?" said a voice behind us.

We spun around and stared into the grinning face of a teenaged boy, his hair bleached to straw, his chest burned brown from the sun.

As I met his gray eyes, I was painfully aware of my sloppy appearance and B.O. I probably smelled worse than Henry Bockelman at Second Time Around. "I—I hope you don't mind. We were so thirsty."

"No problem," he said as he drew himself a drink.

"Thanks for the water. We'd better go."

"What's your hurry? Where you headed? Stick around for a few minutes, and I'll give you a ride."

"Oh, no. We're just picking up cans."

"Good for you. You wouldn't believe the junk people dump out here in the country. Jim Norfleet's my name. What's yours?"

"Uh, this is Jackson," I said, "and I'm—Jo."

"When I first saw you from the hayfield, I thought you might be those two kids who ran away from Gabriel."

"Gabriel who?" asked Jackie, dead-pan. I could have hugged him.

Jim chuckled. "Not who—what. Gabriel's a town north of here."

"Runaways, huh?" I said. "Boys or girls?"

"One of each."

"Oh. We'll keep our eyes open."

✦

A chimney stood tall and lonely against the sky. Drawing closer, I saw it was joined to the crumbling foundation of a house that had burned to the ground. In the yard sat an old-fashioned pump on a slab of concrete. I ran to the pump and started working the handle up and down.

Jackie's eyes nearly popped out of his head when water gushed from the pump's mouth and splashed onto the slab. "All ri—ight," he squealed, plunging his head into the flow.

We filled the jugs with the icy water, and I emptied one over my head. "Brrr. Cold shower. . . . Hey, you know what? We could take baths. Fill the wagon with water and let it warm up in the sun."

"I don't want a bath. I want to play fort over there," said Jackie, pointing to the foundation.

"You can do both. See that old barn? We're going to spend the night here."

✦

Jackie bathed first, undisturbed by the herd of black Angus cows ogling him across a fence. I didn't like having an audience, so I washed myself quickly and got out. As I pulled on a pair of shorts and the Gremlins T-shirt, I wondered if the shirt really had belonged to Lydia Barton.

I rinsed our dirty clothes and hung them on the fence, then carried our sleeping bags to the barn loft. I was opening a door to let in some air when I saw Jim Norfleet's pickup coming up the road, kicking up dust.

Too late—because the truck was slowing down—I thought of our laundry hanging out in the open. I scrambled down from the ladder and peered through a crack in the boards. Jackie was hunkering down in his fort, and the truck was pulling into the yard.

Had Jim come looking for us? If so, he'd see that I was wearing a shirt that advertised "Gabriel Gremlins."

Jim stopped at the fence, opened a gate, and drove into the pasture. I let out my breath. Obviously, he was checking on the cattle.

I motioned for Jackie to stay put. Several minutes

passed before Jim finished his chores and left, but when the coast was clear, Jackie hollered, "That was fun. I pretended Jim was the enemy."

"He is. Everybody's our enemy as long as we're on the run."

I read *To Kill a Mockingbird* until my stomach started rumbling, then went to the wagon and got the box of saltine crackers. I'd been holding off on them because they'd make us thirsty, but now we had a well and all the water I could haul up out of the ground.

When I went to the door to tell Jackie to come and eat, Jim Norfleet's pickup was turning into the drive again. I retreated into the shadows of the barn.

Jim got out of the truck, carrying a cardboard box, which he set down on the concrete slab by the pump. "Chow time," he called, looking all around. "My mom's feeding the hay crew, so she won't miss this fried chicken."

Fried chicken! My mouth watered at the thought, but I was afraid this was a trap.

Jim returned to the truck. "I don't know if you guys are runaways or what, but your secret's safe with me," he said, then got in and drove away.

As soon as the pickup was out of sight, Jackie and I made a run for the box and tore into it. We found golden fried chicken, still hot and wrapped in foil, a whole cherry pie, and two cans of cold Pepsi.

We ate all the chicken and half the pie and swigged down the soft drinks. When we were finished, Jackie crushed his can underfoot and let out a satisfied burp. "If we have to have enemies," he said, "I hope they're all like Jim Norfleet."

✦

I fell asleep to the sound of doves cooing in the barn loft. When a rooster crowed at daybreak, I stretched lazily and looked out the window. The sun glowed brilliant orange as it peeked through the trees, giving the illusion of a forest fire.

I listened to the morning as it came alive with birds. A wild turkey gobbled. A blue jay called once and its mate answered. A woodpecker hammered away at a tree trunk.

Free as a bird, I thought. At Truman Lake, we'll be free as a bird.

I knew we couldn't stay in a public campground, like we had with Leonard and Mama. But the lake had miles and miles of shoreline, with marinas and a few houses and lots of wilderness. I wanted to find an isolated place to set up camp and yet be fairly close to the business area. If we could blend in with the tourists, nobody would be the wiser.

We finished off the cherry pie for breakfast, and I washed the pie pan and left it in the box for Jim to pick up. By seven o'clock, we were on our way.

Although we started out ready to whip the world, that didn't last long. The road stretched out before us—an endless dirty ribbon, strung between parched weeds. We moved like robots, mechanically placing one foot in front of the other.

The blazing sun turned the gravel into hot coals and heated our drinking water. Our salvation came at cattle feedlots, where cool, fresh water flowed from pipes into stock tanks. Once, when I was guzzling a drink, Jackie stepped in a pile of gooey green stuff.

"Gross," he grumbled, scraping his shoe on a rock.

"Lesson one in farming," I said drily. "He who walks in fresh, hot cow manure is destined to stink all day."

When cars passed us, the drivers either honked and waved or stopped and offered us rides, which we refused. Each time, as a good Samaritan moved on, I'd shake my head in disbelief. Had no one heard news reports of runaways?

That night, we found shelter in a junked car in a fence row. Before it got too dark to see, I climbed into the backseat and sorted through our food. Eight cookies, a few Cheerios, five slices of bread, ten potatoes, and the crackers.

"I'm starving," said Jackie. "I wish we had some spaghetti."

I looked up at him, hanging over the front seat and still smelling of cow manure. He was dirty and sunburned, his eyes bloodshot. He needed a bath, some lotion, and a nourishing meal. I couldn't give him those things, but I could spice up what we had with a little imagination. "Turn around so you can't see what I'm doing."

He obeyed, and I peeled and rinsed a potato. "Now close your eyes and hold your nose." I fed him the potato, a slice at a time, all the while giving him a pep talk. "Pretend this is a nice, juicy apple. It's crunchy. It's sweet. So chew it slow."

When the potato was gone, he said, "Apples are OK, but I'd rather have spaghetti."

13
TRUMAN LAKE

The next day—Friday—was a blur of heat and dust and thirst. Just when I thought I couldn't take another step, we came to a crossroads and a crudely lettered sign: "Gas, cold pop, live bait—Rattlesnake Run." If I'd had the strength, I'd have leaped for joy. Live bait meant we were nearing Truman Lake.

Rattlesnake Run consisted of a half-dozen houses, a weedy railroad track, a gas station, and a shaggy dog napping in the middle of the road. We entered the station, where country music was blaring from a radio and the odor of motor oil was nauseating in the heat.

"What'll you have?" asked an old man, chewing on a toothpick.

"Two root beers, please. Ice cold."

He served us from a refrigerator that had soft drinks at the top and worms at the bottom.

"How much?"

"A dollar."

As I handed over the money, I asked, "How far is the lake?"

"Just a hoot and a holler down the road."

Outside, I looked at the map and calculated a hoot and a holler to be half a mile or less.

It was almost three o'clock when the faint fishy smell of Truman Lake tantalized us with the promise of a cool dip. At every bend in the road, Jackie ran ahead to look. Finally, he disappeared over a rise and didn't come back.

When I topped the hill, I caught my breath as I surveyed the cove before me. Where the road ended, the water began—calm blue water the exact shade of the sky.

Jackie was splashing for all he was worth and yelling at me to hurry up. I parked the wagon, then ran down the hill and plunged in. Lying back, I floated dreamily, lulled by the distant droning of speedboats in the open channel.

I knew the lake was man-made by the U.S. Army Corps of Engineers, but to my tired eyes it was every bit as magnificent as the oceans God formed at the beginning of time. Trees rose from the water, their spindly arms reaching upward like drowning men.

Drowning men? My head shot up. "Jackie!" I said, rolling over.

"Hey, Freed, come look at this giant crawdad."

I swam over to the shallows and watched the crawdad scuttling over the rocks. It was magnified by the clear water, and its pincers looked wicked.

"Are crawdads good to eat?" Jackie asked.

"Beats me. Now that we've cooled off, we'd better be moving on."

"What's wrong with right here?"

I motioned toward the speedboats. "Too much traffic. A tent in this place would show up like a toad in a punch bowl."

We went back up the gravel road and turned left onto a blacktop. A few minutes later, we stood on a bridge and stared down at a roped-off swimming area jam-packed with tourists. Naturally, Jackie wanted to run right down and join them, but I wouldn't let him.

"Why not?" he demanded. "The sign says it's free."

"We've got to find a place of our own, private but near a public campground, so we can get drinking water and take showers when we want."

His eyes widened. "You think we can get away with that?"

"Sure. Mom and Leonard used to sign in with the caretaker, and then we were free to come and go as we pleased."

On up the highway, we came to a sign that said "Camping" and followed it down a gravel road to the entrance of a campground called Sleepy Shoals. The gatehouse was empty. We could have walked in unnoticed, but we passed on by.

About a quarter mile beyond the Sleepy Shoals entrance was a dirt road overgrown with weeds and vines.

"Let's see where this goes," I said. "Looks like nobody's used it for years." Not even snakes, I hoped.

It was a struggle, hauling the wagon down that path. When at last we reached the shoreline, we were breathing hard and soaked with sweat.

The sun was sparkling on the water so that it hurt

my eyes to look. I shaded them and peered across the lake, at the speedboats churning up a froth. On the far side of the channel, fishing boats drifted alongside a bluff, but our side was deserted, with dead treetops jutting from the water between us and a small island about fifty yards out.

Jackie splashed into the lake and began scouting for more crawdads.

I kicked off my shoes and waded out up to my neck. Another step, and my head went under. Slimy branches clawed at my feet like the tentacles of an octopus. I shot to the surface and gasped air. As I dog-paddled back to shore, I warned Jackie, "Those underwater trees are dangerous. Don't go out any farther than you are right now."

"I'm a good swimmer."

"Just do as I say, or you might end up as fish bait."

I had sand in my shorts, so I slipped behind a tree and changed into dry clothes. After rinsing the grit from my wet ones, I slung them over a branch to dry and sat down to read the instructions for putting up the tent. They looked simple enough, but when I began trying to extend the expandable poles, the aluminum sections wouldn't slide. I pulled, I twisted, I grunted. Nothing worked.

"What's the matter?" asked Jackie.

"These stupid poles won't come apart."

He fiddled with one and pried off its cap with a knife. When he jammed a stick into the open end and pulled, the pole telescoped out with a screech.

"You really are the brains of this outfit," I said.

He helped me extend all the poles, but they wouldn't connect to each other until we'd routed out their ends with a stick and greased them with lard. We soon discovered that the ground was hard as concrete, and we had to use a rock to pound in the stakes. By the time we got that tent up, I hated it with a passion.

My stepfather's voice echoed in my mind, telling me that lake animals are used to the smell of humans and they'd come right into the camp to get food. "We'll need lots of firewood," I said. "It'll turn chilly here by the water when the sun goes down." Leonard had stored our groceries in a metal garbage can, but I planned to keep a fire burning at night to scare away any varmints.

After we'd combed the shoreline for sticks that were small enough to carry and dry enough to burn, we dragged in a driftwood log to serve as our table and chairs.

I hadn't noticed how the time had zipped by. When the sun dropped out of sight behind the trees, darkness fell all at once. The air turned cool, causing an eerie mist to rise from the lake.

The mosquitoes found us, so I built a fire to smoke them out and cook our supper. I almost smoked myself out, too, and the heat was agony against my sunburn.

While the potatoes were cooking, I put our cookies, crackers, and remaining potatoes on a stump, turned the wagon upside down over it, and weighted it with rocks.

We ate with our jackets on and stared out over the

black water. The trees behind us came alive with
creatures flapping and hooting in the darkness. A
clicking sound that I imagined was a scorpion dragging its tail turned out to be the crackling of the fire.
Still, I kept glancing back over my shoulder, feeling
trapped.

I wondered why I wasn't happier about reaching
our destination. Although we were safe from Miss
Harbaugh and the Child Protection Agency, I didn't
feel at all safe in this wilderness.

It was strange. I hadn't feared the wild when I'd
been camping with Mama and Leonard, but now that
Jackie and I were on our own, I was spooked. I wished
we had a boat so we could ferry our belongings to the
island. There we'd be more or less protected by water
on all sides.

When Jackie finished eating, he yawned and cud-
dled up close to me for warmth. "I'm glad we don't
have to do any more walking," he said.

"But we do. Tomorrow we've got to buy groceries."

He sighed contentedly. "Peanut butter and jelly and
fresh bread."

14

LANCE B. WOOLCOTT

⭐ A howling sound woke me in the middle of the night, and I sat straight up in my sleeping bag, thinking it was wolves. It was only the wind. A few raindrops plopped onto the tent and rolled off with a "pfffffft." Thunder rumbled, and the tent lit up for an instant as the sky flickered with lightning. A storm was coming. Great. Just great.

I hurried out to douse the campfire so its sparks wouldn't set the countryside ablaze, but the dried wood must have burned up in no time because there was nothing. Not even the tiniest coal glowed in the darkness. "So much for scaring off wild animals," I muttered as I felt my way back into the tent and zipped the flap shut.

A minute later, the sprinkle of rain turned into a torrent. At least our tent doesn't leak, I thought, snuggling down into my sleeping bag. But as the rain pounded and the wind whipped, I remembered that Missouri thunderstorms are notorious for spawning tornadoes. I pictured the tent being hurled into the lake and us drowning, as helpless as kittens in a gunnysack.

I slipped my hand under the edge of the sleeping bag and rubbed it back and forth, but it didn't have the same soothing effect as stroking beneath the mattress at home.

The sound of all that water made me have to go to the bathroom, so I crawled out of the bag—and stepped in an icy puddle. Surely the lake couldn't have risen so quickly! Groping around in the darkness, I opened the tent flap and touched the ground outside. Muddy, but not flooded. We'd either sprung a leak or water was seeping up through the floor.

Lightning zapped directly overhead, terrifying me as I made my nature call. Teeth chattering, feet muddy, I dashed back to the tent and climbed into my sleeping bag. My stomach started hurting, and I lay in a knot, cowering at the violence of the storm.

Jackie remained a softly snoring lump. After a while, I stretched out my legs, but the end of my bag was soaked. Cold and miserable, I drew my knees up to my chest. I fought back tears as I wished the summer away and Mama home again. I hadn't realized until this moment just how much I loved and needed her. Did she feel the same about me?

What was in that letter that had upset her Saturday morning? A threat from a bill collector? Or from Leonard? Was he planning to take Jackie away? And who was the stranger who'd made her cry on the Fourth of July?

Endless hours passed with nothing to keep me company but my own tortured thoughts and the storm. Squeezing my eyes shut, I lay rigid as thunder boomed and lightning exploded like dynamite.

Somehow, I made it through the night, and by daylight, the worst of the storm had passed. The rain had turned to a drizzle.

Pulling on my jacket, I stepped outside into a campsite littered with leaves and limbs and sticks. I found my shirt and shorts and bra in the mud and strung them back over their branch to get washed. My underpants had vanished. The wagon had been pushed aside, the rocks scattered, and our food replaced by animal droppings. I shook my head in disgust. I'd have to buy a garbage can.

When I spotted something white bobbing in the lake, I felt my spirits rise. It was a big slab of Styrofoam, the kind used for floating docks. I fished it out and jammed it into the fork of a tree.

The screech of Styrofoam against wood startled Jackie. "Freedom?" he yelped. "What was that?"

Dripping and shivering, I crawled back into the tent. "Our own little ferry boat. Now we can move our gear to the island."

"Is it raining?"

"Yeah, and an animal stole our food."

We read and played rummy until noon, and still it rained. I developed a headache from not eating, and Jackie became a broken record of complaints: "I'm cold. . . . I'm bored. . . . I'm hungry. . . ."

I picked up Mama's yearbook, and my spelling bee clipping fell out. "Freedom reigns on the Fourth of July." I smiled and put it back, then thumbed through the book, reading the names of the students pictured there. When the face of Josie Ann Avery jumped out at me, goose bumps raised on my arms. She'd been my age when she burned to death. Two grades over was a smiling, freckle-faced boy who looked a lot like Jackie. Thomas Jackson Avery, Mama's brother. Dead at fifteen.

Hastily, I flipped ahead to the senior pictures and found Mama's. She was prettier than her classmates, I decided as I compared her to the other girls. Five pages over, a boy's picture caught my attention because it was autographed. Lance B. Woolcott had scrawled in red ink, "All my love always, Lanny B."

Lanny. What a sissy nickname for a guy as nice looking as Lance. His hair was dark and wavy, and he had sparkling eyes. Obviously, he was an old boyfriend of Mama's.

A light came on in my head. An old boyfriend! My father, maybe? I stared at Lance's picture until I'd practically bored a hole into the page. Lance—his name conjured up images of shields and flashing swords. A knight in shining armor, slugging a reporter.

At the end of the yearbook were more messages, and I searched through them, hoping for another one from Lance. Instead, I found the usual "best wishes" from Wynona, Lisa, Carol, and Dorothy, and this one from Marty Q: "What a Fourth of July this was! I thought you were kidding when you threatened to throw that ring into the Lake of the Ozarks. Maybe someday, a hundred years from now, a diver will find it, and he'll wonder how it got there. But we'll never tell!"

"I don't care if I get wet," said Jackie belligerently.

"What?" I said, glancing up to see him standing over me with a stubborn look on his face.

"I'm starved. I want something to eat."

"We'll freeze if we get wet, and we might even get sick."

"I think I'm already sick. My stomach feels awful."

"We don't know where to find a store, and whatever we'd buy would get soaked. We've just got to wait it out."

Jackie threw himself onto his sleeping bag and lay there pouting. In a few minutes, he was asleep.

I lay down, too, with my hands behind my head and the yearbook open on my chest. As I stared up at the sagging roof of the tent, I did some serious thinking about Lance B. Woolcott. How could I locate him? And if I found him, what would I say?

Although my head was splitting, I finally dropped off to sleep. When I awoke, it was after three o'clock and still raining. My clothes, my sleeping bag, even the air in the tent were saturated with dampness. I had the shakes from hunger.

Sleepy Shoals campsite couldn't be more than a quarter mile away along the shoreline. If I could reach its laundry room, I could buy candy and soda pop from its vending machines. Not much of a meal, but better than nothing.

I dug around in the clothes basket for our money sock and woke Jackie and told him where I was going. "Don't leave the tent," I said as I picked up an empty milk jug. "I'll be back as soon as I can."

Icy needles of rain stabbed my body, and clay mud

sucked at my shoes. When I reached the campground, I passed a few tents and camper trucks, but I saw no one. That gave me a weird feeling. Were Jackie and I the only humans left on the planet?

Like the campsites I'd been to before, the main road of Sleepy Shoals was a blacktop that formed a circle. In the center of the circle were the bathhouses, the laundry room, the playground, and a small set of bleachers where the caretaker showed movies at night.

The laundry room was empty, but warm and fresh-smelling from soap. At the vending machines, I exchanged three one-dollar bills for quarters and bought four candy bars and two sodas. They fit into a fairly clean plastic bag I rounded up from a trash can. After filling my water jug at the sink, I trudged out again into the rain.

✦

There wasn't a dry twig anywhere, so Jackie and I didn't even try to build a fire that night. Just before dark, we ate the last candy bar, brushed our teeth, and zipped ourselves into the tent.

I curled up in my sleeping bag, but thoughts of Lance B. Woolcott kept me awake. How could I find out if he was my father? In the twilight zone before sleep, I imagined him riding in on a white horse and proclaiming, "I've come to fill the hole in your soul."

Jackie's voice brought me back to reality. "Freedom, I'm scared. It's so dark." His voice was quivery, like he could cry any minute.

I reached out and took his hand.

"What's going to happen to us?" he asked, posing the same question I'd been pondering for hours.

"Let's not talk about it now. Let's try to get some sleep."

The truth was, I didn't have a clue. This camping business wasn't turning out like I'd planned, and I'd begun to think that running away had been a terrible mistake.

✦

I woke up burning with the desire to call Effie. I told myself it was just to let her know we were all right, but what I really wanted was information about Lance.

A distant church bell reminded me it was Sunday. I unzipped the tent and peeked out at the misty morning. The sun was a shimmering yellow ball on the horizon, and it would make short work of the fog.

Jackie crawled out of his sleeping bag. "Did it stop raining?"

"Yes, thank goodness."

"Can we buy groceries now?"

"You bet your boots," I said, pulling on soggy tennis shoes that would never see white again.

I counted out forty-two dollars, then squirreled away the remaining sixty-five dollars in a hole in the driftwood log. After slinging our sleeping bags over some bushes to dry out, we started up the overgrown path.

"Don't we need the wagon?" asked Jackie.

"No. Wild horses couldn't make me drag it up this hill."

My damp shoes rubbed blisters on both heels, and the half hour it took to reach the highway felt more like half a day.

At an outdoor flea market, where we stopped to ask directions, I spied a big blue enamel cooker with a lid—the kind Effie used to can tomatoes. It was just what we needed for storing groceries and washing laundry. I dickered the price down to a dollar and bought it, and we headed on down the highway.

Soon the delicious, greasy aroma of hamburgers and french fries wafted toward us from the Hilltop Shopping Center. It had a market, a real estate office, a clinic, a drugstore, and a cafe with a pay telephone on its outside wall.

We went to the drugstore first, where we bought flashlight batteries and a roll of nylon rope for a total of six fifty. At Little Piggy's Market, we stuffed the kettle into a cart and filled it with powdered milk, peanut butter, jelly, potatoes, Spam, detergent, bread, and half a dozen cans of vegetables.

The checker showed no particular interest in us as we paid the bill of twenty dollars and sixty-nine cents and got some extra quarters.

Jackie and I left the store, lugging the cooker between us. When we reached the pay phone, I stopped and told him I was going to call Effie.

"Can I talk to her?" he asked.

"No, we don't have much money. I just want to tell her we're OK and . . . ask her something." At his look of disappointment, I added, "But you can listen in."

I lined up seven quarters on the shelf and dialed Effie's number. The operator came on the line and told me to deposit a dollar and a half for the first three minutes.

I was still dropping in quarters when Effie answered, "Hello? Hello, who is this? I can't hear you. What's all that racket?"

"Effie, it's Freedom," I said, holding the receiver away from my ear so Jackie could hear, too.

"Mercy sakes, child! Where are you?"

It was heaven to hear her voice, to get a little taste of home.

"Are you hurt? Sick? Are you in St. Louis? What about all the maniacs—"

"We're fine. I can't tell you where we are, except that we're not in the city. I have to ask you something. Do you know a man named Lance B. Woolcott?"

"Woolcott? What's he—? Did he have something to do with your running away?"

"No, no, he doesn't even know us. But I want to know who *he* is. Please, Effie, think hard."

"I don't have to think. I know who he is. He's a priest."

A priest? After the way he'd signed Mama's yearbook? My hand tightened on the receiver. "Effie, were he and Mama sweethearts when they were in high school?"

"They were. After they broke up, he went off and married the church."

"Where is he now?"

"New York City, last I heard, running a mission for the homeless."

A noble deed for a man named Lance. "What about Miss Harbaugh?" I asked, afraid to ask and afraid not to.

"She's running herself ragged looking for you. Got the police and the sheriff's departments out, too. Your pictures were on TV the other night."

My heart started thudding in my chest.

"Freedom, why don't you give up and come on home?"

"We can't. Not yet. Does Mama know we ran away?"

"No, and I've been praying she doesn't find out. Mary Margaret never was one to handle stress."

"Your three minutes are up," said the operator. "Please signal when through."

"I've got to go, Effie. I'm almost out of change."

"Wait, child!"

" 'Bye," called Jackie as I hung up the receiver.

He was staring at the phone, and I could read his mind. He wanted to return to Gabriel, to take our chances with Miss Harbaugh. But we couldn't. We'd been gone only five days, and we had another twenty-five to go.

"Who is this Lance guy?" he asked finally.

"Just somebody Mama knew a long time ago."

"How'd you find out about him?"

"From the yearbook. I think he was crazy about her back then. I wanted to find out what happened, why they didn't get married. Now I know. He's a priest, and he's married to the church." I felt empty inside, but I tried to shrug it off with a laugh. "He really is a father."

"Huh?"

"With Catholics, father is a title. It's like us calling our minister Brother Bob."

"Oh. For a minute there, I thought you meant Lance was your dad."

15

THE COPPERHEAD

Freedom Jo Avery. Freedom Jo Woolcott. The names kept turning over in my mind. As Jackie and I trudged along the highway with the groceries, I argued with myself.

Why not write to Lance? *Forget it. The man's a priest.*

But maybe he'd want to know he has a daughter. *Why should he? It would only botch up his life.*

At the campsite, we sat down to eat peanut butter and jelly sandwiches. I was still debating the issue of Lance when I noticed an extra set of footprints in the mud. Jackie's and my tennis shoes were worn slick on the bottom, but these were man-sized prints with ridges.

I jumped up, knocking over the jar of peanut butter, and made a beeline for the tent. I flung clothes this way and that until I decided nothing had been stolen.

Snatching up the yearbook, I backed from the tent. It was bad enough that our pictures had been shown on TV. What if someone had seen the yearbook with my clipping in it?

"What's the matter?" asked Jackie.

I pointed at the footprints.

"Ohhh," he said, his eyes big and round and fearful. "Who would have been messing around here?"

"I don't know. The water patrol. The conservation agent. Maybe just somebody snooping." I sat down and examined the clipping, as if somehow I could tell whether a stranger's eyes had read it. "We've got to move our camp," I said, scowling at the tent we'd have to take down and put up again.

"Where?"

"To the island. Nobody can sneak up on us out there."

We swam out and explored the island, which was about half the size of a football field and dense as a jungle with trees and tangled vines. After selecting a site near the open channel, we traveled back and forth, floating our gear on the Styrofoam ferry. Fortunately, the tent came apart easily, and went back up without a hitch.

When at last we had everything situated, I tied a rope to the cooker full of groceries and swung it from a tree. It would take a mighty tall 'coon to reach it now.

That evening, Jackie and I sat by the fire, listening to the chugging of boats and watching their lights trace patterns on the lake. The water slapping the shore made a pleasant sound, like liquid laughter, and for the first time since we'd left home, I could relax and enjoy Mother Nature.

✦

The next day was a blue Monday. My head throbbed, my stomach hurt, and I was so cranky, I couldn't get along with myself. By suppertime, I was so down in the dumps, I needed a shovel to dig myself out. I broke the tab on the Spam can trying to open it, and when I tried to pry the lid off with a stick, I sliced a princess pinkie. "Ouch!" I yelped, throwing down the can to nurse my injury.

Jackie picked up the Spam and started fooling with the lid.

"Leave that alone!" I snapped. "You'll cut your hand off!"

He blinked at the harshness in my voice. "I just wanted to help."

"I know. I'm sorry." To my surprise, I burst into tears.

He stared at me in horror. "Freed, what's the matter?"

"I don't know," I sobbed. "I just can't think straight."

Eventually, I pulled myself together and worked the Spam lid back and forth until half of it broke off. We ate chunks of the meat and green beans for supper.

Later, while making a nature call in the woods, I discovered blood on my underwear. "The troops have landed," I muttered, borrowing Alice's expression. It was my first period, which explained the bad mood and stomachache.

Although I'd had sex education in health class, I

wasn't prepared for my own visit from the troops. I hurried to the tent and sorted through the laundry basket to find something that would work for a pad. A sock with a hole in the heel was the best I could do. When that was in place, I went out and sat on the log to think.

The troops were really rolling now, but it would soon be dark and the market was closed. What had pioneer women used for pads when they were heading West? An old dish towel? A hanky? Buckskin?

From Sleepy Shoals came a muffled burst of laughter. The campground. Surely there'd be a vending machine in the ladies' shower room. At the very worst, I could ask around and find a woman who had some pads.

I got up, trying to ignore the cramping in my gut, and went looking for Jackie.

He was racing acorn boats in the shallows, and he didn't want to stop, especially when I said we were going to the campground to take showers. "But I'm not dirty," he objected.

"Your hair is. It hasn't seen shampoo since we left home. Besides, wouldn't you like to watch a movie?"

"What?"

"The camp has free movies at night. Shows like *Old Yeller*."

"I guess I'd take a shower for that."

We ferried our clean clothes and toiletries across the water and walked along the shoreline. On the way to the asphalt circle, we passed tents and camper trucks and two Winnebagos. People of all ages were milling about, barbecuing and telling fish stories. They gave us no more than a casual glance, but the aroma of their hot dogs, hamburgers, and steaks made my stomach roll over and beg.

"Hoo, boy," Jackie said, breathing deep. "That sure doesn't smell like Spam."

✦

Scrubbed and shampooed and concealing extra pads for the troops in my bundle of dirty clothes, I left the ladies' shower room. As soon as I cleared the door, Jackie grabbed my arm and hissed, "Boy Scouts from Gabriel. I saw Stevie Meyers and Ricky Stidwell getting water from the hydrant."

"Did they see you?"

"You think I'm dumb or something?"

"No, I— We've got to get away from here." I glanced around frantically. "This way," I said, starting up the road toward the gatehouse. "We'll have to go the long way around, through the woods."

It was dark by the time we reached the turnoff. When I directed the flashlight at the tangled path, my imagination kicked into high gear, conjuring up scorpions and snakes.

Jackie picked up a big stick and clutched my arm in a death grip. "I sure wish we could have seen *Old Yeller*."

"Me, too," I said, and plunged with him into the wilderness.

Low branches reached out to trip us, while high ones caught in our hair. Creatures screeched and hooted. A deer crashed through the woods, terrifying us, but we kept going. My heart was still racing when I sensed something that raised the hairs on the back of my neck. A smell like wet moss or rotten bark.

"Stop!" I croaked.

We stopped, and I scoured the ground with the beam of light. When I saw a head, bright as a penny, and eyes like vertical slits, the blood turned to ice in my veins. It was a copperhead, coiled to strike.

"Now!" I yelled, hurling the flashlight at the snake as I threw my weight against Jackie.

We landed in a heap, scattering wet towels and dirty clothes in all directions. A few feet away lay the flashlight, shining upward on empty space.

Praying that the snake would be long gone, I fished for the light with Jackie's stick. As I turned the beam on my little brother's face, I realized he hadn't made a sound. "Are you all right?"

"My leg. It's hurt."

Fear tied a knot in my throat. Had the copperhead struck him?

"I fell on a rock."

Lowering the light, I saw a long, deep gash in his calf and blood running down into his sock. "Oh, Jackie. Does it hurt really bad?"

"Not too bad. I can walk on it. Shoot, I can *run* on it. Let's get out of here."

I wiped his leg with a towel and snatched up our things. "Are you sure you can run?"

"I'm sure. Let's go!"

We hightailed it through the woods so fast our feet

barely touched the ground. When we reached the clearing, Jackie's leg was still bleeding. I had him sit down while I bandaged it with one of my troop pads. He didn't ask what it was or where it came from, and I didn't offer an explanation.

Jackie aimed the flashlight while I ferried him to the island, avoiding the dead trees that hovered over us like skinny witches. The water was warm and black as ink.

When we reached the shallows, I stood up and pushed the Styrofoam to ground, only then remembering that I'd forgotten to take my shoes off. Soggy shoes and blisters, again.

At the campsite, I checked Jackie's bandage and saw that the bleeding had stopped. "OK now?" I asked.

"I think so." He was shivering, even though it wasn't cold and I was the one who was wet.

I stroked his hair and said, "You'd better go to bed."

He went without an argument. I changed into dry clothes, then built a fire and sat staring into the flames for a long, long time. That copperhead could have bitten one of us, as easy as not. I pictured those fangs sinking into soft flesh . . . and started shaking uncontrollably. I was desperate for the thirty days to be over, so we could go back home.

16
WANTED: DEAD OR ALIVE

Jackie raved about snakes in his sleep, and twice he tried to kill the clothes in our basket. By morning, his leg was so sore he could barely walk.

After breakfast, when I removed the bandage, the cut started bleeding again. It was puffy and the skin all around was tinged with pink, and I knew it needed medical attention. I went straight to the driftwood log and started withdrawing money from the sock.

"What's that for?" Jackie asked.

"I'm taking you to the clinic."

"I don't want to see a doctor. He'll sew me up, and it'll hurt."

"He'll deaden your leg, so you won't feel a thing." The doctor's bill is what'll hurt, I thought, as I counted our money—seventy-six dollars and some change.

"What if we see those Gabriel guys at the shopping center?"

"Boy Scouts don't come to the lake to shop. They come to swim and fish."

Jackie tried his weight on his injured leg and

winced. "Freed," he said, "I don't think I can make it."

I smiled at his last-ditch effort to escape the doctor. "I'll take you in the wagon."

"You said wild horses couldn't make you pull it up the hill."

I gave him a quick hug and murmured, "But little brothers can. Come on. I'll help you to the water's edge, then ferry you across."

My shoes were still wet, so I didn't bother to remove them for the swim. When we reached the opposite shore, I didn't change my wet clothes, either, but I did hide in the bushes to change my pad. There was no way around it. I was going to have to buy more.

Somehow, I managed to haul the wagon up the hill, and with every step I was scared spitless I'd step on a snake. When I reached the road at last, I stopped to give my blistered feet a rest and pushed strands of wet, lanky hair behind my ears.

"What's my name?" asked Jackie.

I spun around and stared at him, afraid infection had put him out of his head. "What?"

"My name. I can't just tell the doctor I'm Jackie Ramsdale. He might have heard it on the radio."

"I hadn't thought of that."

"I'll be Mike Waisner," he said, combining his best friend's first name with Effie's last name.

"And I'll be your sister Effie."

He laughed for a minute, then became sober. "It's not right to lie, especially about somebody as nice as Effie."

I knew what he meant. I sometimes had to stretch the truth in all directions, like when I called in sick for Mama, but I'd never outright lied. "Don't think of it as a lie. Just pretend we're a part of Effie's family."

"I have," he said wistfully. "Lots of times."

When we at last reached the clinic, Jackie sat down in the waiting room, while I attacked the water fountain. I drank and drank and drank, until someone said, "You'll make yourself sick."

I came up for air and saw a heavyset lady with a bushel-basket hairdo, rhinestone-studded glasses, and a pucker of disapproval. According to her name tag, she was Mrs. Agnes Borchers, receptionist. "Sorry, ma'am. I was spitting cotton."

"What can Doctor do for you today?"

I thought about asking if "Doctor" had a name. Instead, I said, "That's my little brother, Mike Waisner. He cut his leg."

"Do you have insurance?"

"No, ma'am. We've got cash."

"Where are your folks? Doctor won't treat minors without parental consent."

Now what? Jackie needed help, and he was going to get it if I had to run right over Mrs. Borchers and corner "Doctor" myself. Out of my mouth came the words, "Our folks are on an all-day fishing trip. We're camping at Sleepy Shoals. You can call there if you like."

Mrs. Borchers removed her glasses and started polishing them on the hem of her skirt.

I held my breath and stared at the red marks on her

nose, willing her not to pick up the phone and make the call.

She replaced the glasses and said, "If your folks aren't available, there's no sense calling for permission. We'll treat this as we do other emergencies and hope we don't get sued. Is your brother allergic to any medication?"

✦

"Doctor" was Doctor Coreen Gann, a small, dark-haired woman who smelled of cloves and antiseptic. Her slacks and shirt, soft and pink as cotton candy, made me self-conscious of our appearance. Jackie was rumpled from sleeping in his clothes, and the blood on his tennis shoe had stained it dark brown. My hair felt like a rat's nest, and my shorts and shirt were grungy, from getting wet, then dusty.

After swabbing Jackie's leg with antiseptic, Doctor Gann asked him to close his eyes and recite the alphabet backwards.

He grunted when the deadening needle went in, but soon he was relaxed. I watched, fascinated, as the doctor stitched the wound.

She talked nonstop to Jackie, asking how he'd gotten hurt, what he wanted to be when he grew up. I thought we were in trouble when she asked where he went to school, but he was way ahead of me.

"George Washington Elementary."

I squeezed his hand for not saying "Gabriel."

"You're a brave little boy, Mike. Twelve stitches and you didn't holler once," Doctor Gann said, clipping the last thread and dropping the scissors into a tray. She placed a big square Band-Aid over the injury. "Keep the leg dry and change the bandage every day."

"You mean I can't swim?" asked Jackie.

"No swimming. Sorry. How long will you be at the lake?"

"Uh, um, why?" I stammered.

"The stitches should be taken out in a week. If you come here, the follow-up is free." Doctor Gann gave me a prescription for an antibiotic, then walked with us to the front desk. She whispered something to Mrs. Borchers before disappearing down the hall.

"Your bill comes to ten dollars," said the receptionist with a frown.

Ten dollars? The sign behind her said office visits were twenty-five. Suddenly, I felt shame burning through my cheeks. Doctor Gann considered us a charity case.

"I thought you said you had cash," said Mrs. Borchers. Her eyes glittered behind the rhinestones, and I felt she was ridiculing me.

I flashed her a toothy smile. With deliberate slowness, I pulled out my whole roll of seventy-six dollars and peeled off twenty-five, saying, "We'll pay the full price, the same as everybody else."

✦

At the drugstore, I bought Band-Aids, sanitary pads, and the medicine—almost twenty-two dollars total. When I went up front to get Jackie, he said, "Watch this," and showed me he could work a yo-yo.

"You want that?" I started to hand him some

money, but my hand froze in mid-air. Our pictures were on the wall with the caption, "Have you seen these children?"

"Will there be anything else?" called the pharmacist.

I forced myself to be calm. "No, thank you. My brother's just trying out yo-yos." To Jackie, I whispered, "Look at the wall."

He looked and turned white, and we slunk out of the store.

"Just like in the movies," he said, plopping down in the wagon we'd parked on the sidewalk. " 'Wanted: Dead or Alive.' "

"Don't talk for a minute," I said. "I've got to think."

The photographs were last year's school pictures, and they didn't look much like us now. Jackie's hair was shaggy and bleached whiter from so much sun. Mine was a lot longer, and my face was thinner.

An elderly couple walking past gazed at us curiously, and I felt my temperature shoot up a few degrees. "Come on," I muttered. "We'd better stock up on groceries and get out of town."

Our pictures were on the bulletin board at Little Piggy's Market. We sailed through the aisles, grabbing necessities along with some good old junk food—wieners and marshmallows and three packs of Twinkies. If we had to hole up, we'd do it in style.

I left the store with only six dollars and thirty-two cents to my name.

17
SICK AND TIRED

Since Jackie couldn't swim, I didn't, either. We sat tight all that day and the next, racing twig boats, reading, and playing rummy until I was ready to sink into a coma from boredom. Only ten days had passed since Mama left, and twenty more loomed before us. I wondered if a person could die of ennui.

After dark Wednesday, the wind coming off the water was icy. I put on my jacket and told Jackie I was going after drinking water.

"And leave me here?"

"I'm riding the ferry. It's too cold to swim. You've got the campfire, and there's a moon-glade on the water." I pointed to the moonlight dancing on the waves.

"I guess somebody needs to hold down the fort."

I'd expected an argument, and I gaped at him in surprise.

Jackie picked up a club from our stack of firewood. "For the bears," he said. "I'll conk 'em on the head."

"Is that you, Cotton Top? At home you were scared to go down the hall in the dark."

"I decided to be brave, like you when you saved us from the snake. I'm tired of being a scaredy-cat."

I wrapped my arms around him and kissed the top of his head.

"Don't do that," he said. "Kissing's for sissies."

✦

Thursday was what Effie would have called a weather breeder. It was steamy and still, and the leaves on the trees turned bottom side up, as if they were tongues hanging out.

Jackie entertained himself by building a city in the dirt. I did the laundry, then filled the kettle with lake water, so the sun would warm it for sponge baths and shampoos.

Listlessly, I spread my sleeping bag on the ground and lay down to read *A Tree Grows in Brooklyn* for the second time. I couldn't get interested.

By suppertime, the sky threatened rain, and I put our clean clothes away. As I watched the clouds roll in, I felt totally bummed out at the thought of spending another stormy night in the tent. Instead of cooking supper, I began leafing through the yearbook. Mama was still smiling as if she didn't have a care in the world, and Lanny B was still sending all his love always. I slammed the book shut and sat staring off into space.

"Listen!" said Jackie suddenly.

I listened. A motorboat and men's voices, dangerously close.

"Stay here," I said. I darted toward the sounds and

hid behind a tree as two young men in bathing suits beached their boat on our island. They unloaded three big red coolers, then got back into the boat and roared away.

If they were getting ready for a picnic, they must be expecting a crowd. I crept over, lifted the lid of one cooler, and saw it loaded to the brim with beer on ice. I lifted the lid of another cooler. More beer.

My hand was on the third lid when I heard boisterous laughter and singing in the distance. Deep voices. Men's voices. I looked across the water and felt a wave of panic. A dozen men in six canoes were paddling straight toward me.

I ran back to the campsite. Jackie's city was deserted, and I felt my throat tighten. Those canoes were coming fast. "Jackie! Jackie!" I croaked. "Where are you?"

"I'm right here," he said, peeking around from behind a tree. "Can't a guy take a whiz in private?"

"Men coming! We've got to get away! Grab whatever you can, and let's go!"

He picked up his shoes and the peanut butter and ran for the ferry. I snatched up my sleeping bag, the money sock, and the yearbook, and followed him.

We waited until the men had reached the far side of the island, so they wouldn't see us. Then Jackie jumped onto the Styrofoam, and I tossed our belongings onto it and ferried him across the lake.

We beached at our old campsite. No tent, no log to sit on, not even a match so we could start a fire.

I sat down on the ground to pour the water from

my shoes and wring out my socks. I suspected the beer party would last into the wee hours, but we couldn't—wouldn't—spend the night here at the edge of the wilderness, not with scorpions and copperheads and maybe even rattlesnakes.

"What'll we do now?" asked Jackie.

"Sleepy Shoals. The laundry room. As soon as it gets dark." Resentfully, I stared out across the water. My hair was oily, my clothes were soggy, and I wanted my Twinkies.

I'm sick to death of Truman Lake, I thought, and slapped at a mosquito. A bullfrog raised its bulbous eyes above the water line and belched, echoing my sentiments exactly. I was tired of having wet feet. Tired of worrying. Tired of running. Tired of having to make a decision about every little thing.

We ate peanut butter with a stick, while the men on our island laughed and shouted and boozed it up. Smoke drifted across the point, and I knew they'd built a fire. Scowling at the gray-green sky, I wished for a gully washer, so those guys would get good and wet.

At dark, we crept along the shoreline and slipped into the public campground. The air was pungent with the smell of citronella candles lit to shoo the bugs away. Moms and dads at picnic tables looked like floating faces in the glow of lantern light. Children scuttled in a game of squat tag, their voices mingling with the sound of a baby's cry nearby.

It all seemed so ordinary, so pleasant, so homey, even though these people were tourists in a temporary place. They were families on vacation, and they had each other and a home somewhere.

A home somewhere. Not an empty apartment. Not a sleeping bag on a creek bank. Not a tent on an island crawling with drunks. All at once, the hole in my soul was so big and empty, I questioned whether I had a soul at all.

In the laundry room, the air was heavy with the perfume of fabric softener, and a single light burned dimly at the rear. We made our bed on the floor and went to sleep.

When a screaming siren woke me, I shot upright, sure it was the cops come to get us.

"What's the matter?" asked Jackie, rubbing the sleep from his eyes.

From outside came the sound of wind and water. A red light flashed past out front, distorted by the rain on the plate-glass windows. We ran to the door and looked out as a bone-chilling announcement blared from a patrol car: "Tornado warning! Leave your tents and vehicles and take shelter immediately. I repeat. Tornado warning. Take shelter immediately."

Jackie grabbed my arm. "Are we safe here?"

"No. Too many windows."

Before I could think what to do, a horde of people came running toward us. Bigeyed and barefooted, they shot on past, like cockroaches fleeing Raid.

We followed the crowd and ended up at the men's bathhouse. Its concrete block walls magnified the racket of kids crying, and the smell of earthen dampness mingled with that of wet clothes. Everyone was shivering, maybe from cold, maybe from fear. I didn't see any Boy Scouts.

Jackie and I sat on the floor, sharing a corner with a live cricket trapped in a spider web. As soon as the kids got quiet, the lights flickered and went out, and the crying started again. I felt Jackie's cold hand groping for mine. I rubbed it to warm it, then leaned back against the wall.

Eventually, the noise died down, except for a radio that crackled with static. I figured people were either asleep or listening to the storm. I was listening so hard my ears hurt, hoping that the rain and wind wouldn't stop, wouldn't yield to silence. That would be the sign of imminent danger.

How safe is this building? I wondered. Will it survive a tornado, or will it come apart like Tinkertoys? I thought about the cricket, who was bound to die, either way.

A half hour passed, then another. My body was chilled from the concrete floor. My arm was numb from Jackie sleeping against it. When the radio gave the "all clear," I wasn't sure my creaky joints would let me get up.

After easing Jackie away, I stood up, groaning, and stretched. It was still dark, but the groaning and popping in the room told me others were stretching, too.

Reverent voices spoke words of thankfulness and relief. Hushed voices woke children, who got fussy again. Someone opened the door and held it to let in the early-morning light.

"Is it over?" asked Jackie.

Bending down, I freed the cricket from the web.

"It's over," I said as the bug sprang from my fingers in a joyful arc.

✦

The sun was barely peeping over the horizon, as if reluctant to shine upon destruction. Sleepy Shoals was littered with broken limbs, an upended picnic table, a tent wadded up in a tree. But farther down, along the shoreline, pieces of boats, docks, and roofs had literally dropped out of the sky.

On our island, giant trees lay tangled against each other, their black, wet roots torn from the earth. The remains of a pontoon boat perched at a crazy angle on the spot where Jackie had last jumped on the ferry. Unexplainably, a minnow bucket with its lid intact bobbed peacefully in the water amidst a mass of sticks.

"Goll-eee," breathed Jackie.

I knew our camp was wiped out. When I kicked at some red trash and saw it was part of a canoe, I felt nauseated. What had happened to the beer drinkers? I'd wished them good and wet, not dead.

Jackie picked his way through debris at our old campsite and peered into the woods. "Our wagon's gone," he said.

I stared at a stick in the water. No, it wasn't a stick, but a snake. The water was alive with snakes. If snakes could survive a tornado, maybe people could, too.

Jackie pulled on my arm. "Wanna go see about our tent and stuff?"

I shook my head. A patrol boat was approaching.

It came right through the snakes, but stopped short of the floating junk. A man cut the engine and called, "You folks OK?"

"We're OK," I said, "but I don't know about the guys on that island."

"The whole bunch is locked up in the county jail."

"Jail?"

"Minors in possession of alcohol."

I laughed out loud.

18
BACK TO GABRIEL

 "Thank you for calling AT&T. Hold for that number."

Using a chalk rock, I scratched the number on the sidewalk outside Kitty's Cafe, and wondered why every telephone operator I'd ever heard sounded as if she had a clothespin on her nose. I took a deep breath, savoring the aroma of coffee brewing and bacon sizzling. I wanted to remember my last smell of freedom.

My quarters were lined up all in a row. A caterpillar in a fuzzy blond coat was wiggling lazily toward me on the brick wall. Jackie was sitting on the sidewalk, peeling the dirty Band-Aid off his leg.

I dialed the number, and another nasal-voiced operator came on the line to tell me to deposit a dollar fifty.

One quarter, two, three, four, five, six. The phone was ringing.

I stared at the tiny beady eyes of the caterpillar, who would spin a cocoon and someday soar freely into the world as a butterfly. I thought of bare ground beneath a whipping post—nature's way of saying one person should never lay claim against another.

168 ♣ JUNE RAE WOOD

"Child Protection Agency. Hilda Harbaugh."

"Miss Harbaugh, this is Freedom Avery."

"Freedom Avery! What in the world? Where are you? I certainly hope this call means you're ready to come back home."

I swallowed hard. "We're ready to come back to Gabriel, but a couple of beds in a stranger's house don't qualify as a home."

"Have it your way. Now tell me where you are."

"At the Hilltop Shopping Center at Truman Lake."

"That tornado—"

"—went right over our heads."

"Well, that's a miracle."

A miracle? Or just nature's way of saying kids shouldn't try to fool grown-ups?

"I've got fliers at the shopping center," Miss Harbaugh said.

"I know, but we didn't get caught. We just decided it was time to come back."

"Well, I should hope so. Do you know how many people have been looking for you? Worrying about you?"

"Miss Harbaugh, it's just that—I—I didn't want Jackie and me to be separated."

"Well, you can ease your mind about that."

"You've got a foster home that'll take both of us?"

"I've got a place for you both, but it's not exactly a foster home. The judge has ordered a temporary arrangement."

"With Effie?"

"No, with a new couple in town. Now, young lady, give me your exact location."

"Kitty's Cafe."

"I'll be there in an hour."

After hanging up the phone, I tucked the yearbook under my arm and dug our money from the sock. "Take a deep breath," I said to Jackie, "and tell me what you smell?"

He sniffed. "Food?"

"You bet. We're going to Kitty's to pig out on the greasiest hamburgers they've got."

The cafe vibrated with the noise of a jukebox, voices, plates clattering, and a bell dinging orders ready. We sat down at a table cluttered with dirty dishes, which I stacked near the edge.

"Thanks, kids. I'm Fritzi," said the waitress when she stopped beside us to scoop up the plates. "Be back in a minute with the menu."

"All we want is four dollars and eighty-two cents' worth of hamburgers," I said, laying our cash on the table. "However many that will buy."

Fritzi shot me a puzzled glance as she picked up the money and hurried off. Soon she brought us three plates with three hamburgers, the third one cut in half. On her next trip past us, she plopped down two glasses of orange juice, saying, "On the house."

✦

When Hilda Harbaugh stepped from the car, she looked more like a Kool-Aid pitcher than ever. She'd poured herself into a lavender pullover and purple slacks. No, not purple—grape. I vowed never to drink grape Kool-Aid again.

Miss Harbaugh asked if we'd had anything to eat,

then seemed surprised that we had. I guess she expected us to be on the verge of starvation, simply because we looked a little grubby.

I claimed the back seat for myself, but Jackie sat up front and leaned into the vent, letting cool air blow across his face.

"Your running away caused a great deal of trouble in Gabriel," Miss Harbaugh said when we were heading north on the highway. "The police, the sheriff's department, my agency have all been looking for you day and night. Mrs. Waisner's been out of her mind with worry."

I stared at my hands. They were stained and callused, and by no stretch of the imagination could my pinkies belong to a princess.

"Still," continued the social worker, "I understand your fear of being separated. Off the record, I admire your perseverance."

"Does Mama know we ran away?" I asked, picking at the dirt under my fingernails. I desperately needed to take a bath and wash my hair.

"No. We were already doing everything possible to find you, so we decided against telling her. She would have insisted on coming home, and that would have been a mistake."

I started breathing a little easier.

Miss Harbaugh wanted to know all about our stay at the lake and how we'd ended up with little more than the clothes on our backs. I let Jackie do the talking, while I concentrated on watching her face in the rearview mirror and making sure our eyes never met.

Finally, we reached the outskirts of Gabriel. Rubbing a mole on the back of her neck, Miss Harbaugh said, "Let me tell you about the couple who are taking you in. They're Martin and Ona Mae Quincy. They moved here recently to help his sister, who lives in a nice big house in Gabriel."

I didn't care if they had a castle on the Rhine. I'd rather be going to our dinky apartment on Dogwood Lane.

"The Quincys know your mother's in the treatment center, so you don't have to skirt the issue."

Had Miss Harbaugh broadcast that information? Did everybody in the world know Mama was drying out?

"I hope you'll be on your best behavior at the Quincys'. Their making room for you both is an extremely charitable gesture."

Charitable, my eye. They were strangers, taking in somebody else's kids, and they were doing it for the money. I stared out the window as we passed familiar places. The animal shelter, the elementary school, the grocery store, the depot. Suddenly, I sat up straight. We were turning onto Dogwood Lane, and I could see Effie watering her geraniums on the porch.

"I called Mrs. Waisner this morning, to let her know you were all right," said Miss Harbaugh. "She made me promise I'd bring you by, so she could see for herself."

Good, I thought. We can set Effie's mind to rest, and I can get cleaned up.

The car stopped, and Effie came shuffling out to meet us, her faded slippers flopping. A smile lit up her

leathery face, and her false teeth gleamed like porce-
lain.

Jackie and I pushed open our doors and bailed out
running.

"Sakes alive, let me look at the both of you," she
cried as we dove into her outstretched arms.

"Oh, Effie," I breathed and buried my face on her
shoulder.

"What in the world happened? You two look like
orphans," she said, half-laughing, half-crying.

"I missed you," said Jackie.

"And I missed you, child. Both of you."

Miss Harbaugh came clumping up the walk. "We
need to pick up their things and get on over to the
Quincys'. They've been worried, too."

I stiffened. How could total strangers be worried
about somebody they'd never even seen?

Effie patted my back and said to Miss Harbaugh,
"Come on into the house. I've already done their
packing, so you can surely spare a few minutes to let
them scrape some of the dirt off."

At that moment, I loved Effie more than anybody in
the world.

✦

While Jackie was bathing in Effie's bathroom, I went
next door to use ours. I hurried through the house,
trying not to notice how empty it was with Mama
gone.

After my bath, I felt like a different person. Ten
days in the sun had done wonders for me, even if it

hadn't shrunk the bump on my nose. My hair was bleached to the color of corn silks, and my tan had toned down my freckles. There were curves I hadn't noticed before under my plaid shorts and yellow tank top, so I looked more grown up and less gonky.

"You're pretty as a speckled pup," said Effie when I popped back into her apartment. She kissed me good-bye and whispered, "Pretty is as pretty does. Watch your mouth, child, so you won't be getting into trouble."

19
THE QUINCYS

★ "Are you scared?" asked Jackie, when Miss Harbaugh went into the store to buy combs and toothbrushes.

I rested my arm on a box of clothes beside me in the seat. "Scared, no. Just nervous. Some little guy with a jackhammer is working in my stomach."

Jackie nodded, and turned his attention back to the people coming and going at the store.

When Miss Harbaugh came out, she handed me a bag, saying, "Compliments of Mrs. Waisner."

The bag held the necessary toiletries, plus a small bottle of cologne and some rose pink lipstick and nail polish. Bless Effie's heart. She knew Mama wouldn't let me buy makeup.

Miss Harbaugh drove to a subdivision, where neat brick homes with shiny new cars in the driveways spelled "money." I hoped the Quincys didn't live here. I wouldn't know how to act in a house with two fireplaces.

But our destination was at the very edge of the subdivision—an aging two-story house hidden from the street by a row of giant cedars. It had big windows across the front, a swing on the front porch, and a wheelchair ramp beside the steps.

As Jackie and I carried our boxes up the ramp, a slim woman in a green shirt and slacks came to the door. She frisked me with her eyes, as if she thought a runaway would also be a thief.

I checked her out, too—auburn hair to her shoulders, green eye shadow, green eyes.

"Ona Mae," said Miss Harbaugh, "this is Freedom and Jackie. Children, meet Ona Mae."

Everybody said, "Hi," and Ona Mae held the door open.

We stepped into an old-fashioned living room and set our boxes down on a worn hardwood floor that was shiny and pungent from new wax.

"Have a seat," said Ona Mae.

Miss Harbaugh hoisted herself into a chair, while Jackie and I headed for the couch, our grungy tennis shoes squeaking noisily on the floor.

I sat down and glanced around. A quilt appliqued with a farm scene hung on one wall, while more quilts covered the furniture. When I saw a photograph sitting on a table, I did a double take. The girl in the picture was Laura Nell Gentry, of Girl Scout cookie fame.

"So you had an adventure at Truman Lake," said Ona Mae. Although the words were polite, I sensed a coldness in her manner.

"Yeah." I wondered how she was connected to Laura Nell. There was no resemblance that I could see.

Miss Harbaugh said, "I haven't told the children

much about you and Martin. I thought you'd prefer to tell them yourself."

Ona Mae shrugged. "There isn't much to tell. Martin's an insurance adjuster, and I'm a housewife. We have a ten-year-old son, Theodore. We moved back to Gabriel a couple of months ago."

"Where's Theodore?" asked Jackie, and Ona Mae said he was playing ball at the park.

I wanted to ask about Laura Nell, but I sat quietly, popping my knuckles as Ona Mae continued.

"Martin's sister, Helen, has had more than her share of problems, and Martin requested a transfer to Gabriel to help her out. Helen's in a wheelchair, and when her husband died of cancer three years ago, she and her daughter, Laura Nell, moved in here with Grandpa Quincy. Things got to be too much for Helen after Grandpa died in January."

I broke out in a cold sweat. I'd be living under the same roof as Laura Nell Gentry. The girl might look small and wiry, but she was a Mack truck in disguise.

"Have you heard how Mrs. Ramsdale's doing?" asked Ona Mae.

"Not yet," replied Miss Harbaugh, "but we're hoping for the best."

I saw the look that passed between the two women. Did they think Mama's stay at the treatment center was just a waste of time?

At the sound of a vehicle, I glanced outside and saw a van.

"Helen and Laura Nell are back from the therapy center," said Ona Mae. "They go every other day for aquatic therapy."

Laura Nell, dressed in a hot-pink T-shirt and matching shorts, got out of the van and slammed the door. For someone so little, she sure had big hair. It poufed out like a giant brown puffball, dwarfing her pixie face.

Helen was small, too, and frail. After the driver lifted her into a wheelchair and positioned a patch-work quilt over her knees, she pushed a button and wheeled herself up the ramp. When she changed direc-tions, I read the chair's bumper sticker: "Caution: I brake at fabric shops."

"Hi, kids," Helen said as she entered the house. "I'm glad you're here. I hope you'll feel at home."

Laura Nell riveted me with her eyes and gave me a sarcastic grin. "Hello, roommate. We can stay up late every night, talking and eating *cookies*."

I folded my arms over my burning stomach and stifled a groan. Laura Nell hadn't changed a bit.

✦

After Miss Harbaugh left, Ona Mae asked Laura Nell to show Jackie and me our rooms. I felt big and awkward as I followed her up the stairs, carrying our boxes.

Jackie was doubling up with Theodore in a room that had race car coverlets on bunk beds. There wasn't a speck of dirt anywhere, and models, games, cars, and comic books were all lined up on their shelves.

"Hey, wow!" said Jackie, kneeling down to drive a dump truck.

That left me alone with Laura Nell. In the hall, she

smiled wickedly and whispered, "So you ran away from home. I guess I would, too, if my mother was a drunk."

I felt like slapping her pixie face. She'd had some bad breaks, but that didn't give her the right to run over people. If that were the case, I could have flattened half of Missouri myself.

I expected her room to be messy, but it didn't even look lived in, except for the stuffed animals in a net on the ceiling and a few magazines on the floor. The twin beds had matching quilts in a kaleidoscope of colors, and red princess curtains gave the white walls a rosy glow. I was so surprised, I forgot for a moment whose room I was in. "It's beautiful."

Laura Nell snorted. "It's awful. I hate it."

"Why?"

"It's not me. It's a hotel." She swept across the room and threw open the closet, where clothes hung neatly and the shoes were lined up in rows. "Isn't that disgusting? I like a little clutter, some clothes lying around, maybe a few dirty dishes. I had it just like I wanted it, until the inspector showed up."

"The inspector?"

"Uncle Martin. He's a neatness freak, and he expects me to be, too."

I got the picture. With Helen in a wheelchair, the upstairs had been Laura Nell's domain—and probably a pigsty—until the Quincys moved in.

"You'll be sorry you came here. Martin thinks nobody can do anything right but him. If you don't believe me, watch Theodore. He's a nervous wreck.

He messes up playing ball. He can't learn his lines."

"Learn his lines?"

"We're in a play at church for the one hundredth anniversary. He can't memorize."

"How can that be Martin's fault?"

"Just watch. You'll see." Laura Nell began picking up the magazines. "The inspector'll be here for lunch. He's taking the afternoon off, because of you."

"Me?" Did he think I was an axe murderer or something?

"You'd better put your stuff away. I'm giving you the bottom drawer of the chest, the bottom shelf of the book case, and a few inches of rod space in the closet."

I had to force myself not to twirl a finger in the air and say, "Big woop." I set my box on the bed. No way would I open it with her watching. "Your mom seems nice. How long has she been—uh—"

"Crippled? It's not a bad word, you know. She got polio when she was a kid. Mom says Grandpa didn't believe in vaccinations. Uncle Martin says he was too stingy to pay for them."

"Oh. You go to therapy with her?"

"Somebody has to. It's one of their silly rules. Mom doesn't have seizures, but people who do might pull the therapist under water."

Ona Mae called upstairs for Laura Nell to set the table for lunch.

"I'll do it," she said, "and Ona Mae'll come along behind me and redo it. Everything has to be just right for the inspector." She stashed her magazines in the nightstand, but before she left the room, she fired a parting shot. "Don't be nosing around in here while I'm gone."

I gritted my teeth and stared daggers at the empty doorway. How could I stand being cooped up with her for almost three weeks?

After setting my makeup on the bottom shelf of the bookcase, I unpacked my things. Raggedy underwear, two pairs of shorts and a tank top, the shirts I'd bought at the junk store and saved for school. For some reason, Effie had included my spelling trophy and the frilly pink dress I'd worn to the awards ceremony.

The trophy brought back memories of the Fourth of July—my picture in *The Gabriel Gazette,* watching the fireworks from the roof, the stranger arguing with Mama. The Fourth seemed like eons ago.

I set the trophy on the shelf beside the makeup. Its name plate was blank, waiting to be engraved. I wondered what name I'd put there if my father had married Mama. Wouldn't it be something if she came home dry and happy and ready to tell me about him?

A floor board squeaked, and I turned and saw a tall, slender man staring at me from the doorway. I couldn't help but adopt Laura Nell's word for him, because he looked every inch "the inspector": gray business suit, a beak of a nose, wavy black hair graying at the temples, rings on his manicured fingers. I smiled at the thought of bells on his toes.

"You must be Freedom. I'm Martin. Did you find a place for your things?" He swooped in, peered into my open drawer, and touched my pink dress in the closet.

I eased the drawer shut with my foot. The nerve of some people!

Martin straightened his tie and offered me his arm. "I've come to escort a lady to lunch."

Is he some kind of nut? I wondered, but I took his arm and let him escort me down the stairs. We passed through the dining room, where pieces of a jigsaw puzzle were spread out on a round oak table, and went on into the kitchen.

Helen was in her wheelchair at one end of the table. The others—Ona Mae, Laura Nell, and Jackie—were standing behind their chairs. Martin took his place at the head of the table, and I took a seat across from Jackie and Laura Nell.

"Sit down, everyone, before the lasagna gets cold," said Ona Mae. Her voice sounded sharp, as if she were peeved about something.

"Where's Theodore?" asked Martin, eyeing the empty place.

Just then, the back door was flung open and Theodore burst in. "Sorry, Dad. I'll wash up and be right there." He seemed big for ten, all angles and elbows and gonky like me.

As Theodore sidled past us and out of the room, Martin cast him a disapproving glance and said, "Go ahead, Mother. Serve." Ona Mae began dishing up lasagna and passing around the plates.

The lasagna was delicious, but hard to eat daintily because it had big globs of mozzarella cheese. Right off the bat, when I was struggling with a string of cheese that was dangling between my plate and my mouth, I caught Martin eyeing me. I figured he was inspecting my hands, which were stained with a grime that wouldn't wash off.

Theodore slunk into the kitchen, and all eyes turned toward him as he slid into his chair.

Helen said quickly, "I'd like to hear about Truman Lake."

"It was OK, until I hurt my leg," Jackie said. "Then I couldn't swim anymore, and I got bored."

"How'd you get hurt?"

"I fell on a rock. I've still got stitches."

"I guess that means a trip to the doctor," said Ona Mae. "When are the stitches due out?"

"Tuesday," I said.

Ona Mae frowned. "That's my day to help clean the church."

"I'll take him," I said. "We can walk."

"That won't be necessary," said Martin.

"If they can walk thirty-five miles to Truman Lake, they can surely walk across town to the doctor's office," said Ona Mae.

As if she hadn't spoken, Martin turned to Jackie. "I'll close the office an hour early and take you myself. You know, I'd really like to see Truman Lake one of these days. It hadn't been built yet when I was a kid. Maybe I'll take you boys fishing."

I couldn't feature the inspector putting a worm on a hook, but Jackie said, "Hey, neat."

"How about you, son?" Martin asked, looking at Theodore.

Theodore pushed back a lock of unruly hair the same auburn shade as his mother's. "I don't know. Maybe."

"Most boys would jump at the chance to go fishing with their father," said Martin.

"Most boys don't have you for a father," piped Laura Nell.

Martin gave her a withering look, Ona Mae's eyebrows shot up, and Helen hid a smile behind her napkin.

✦

After lunch, Jackie and Theodore went outside to play catch, Laura Nell left to help some second-graders at a day camp, and Martin excused himself to change clothes. I didn't know what to do with myself or even what was expected of me, so when the women began clearing the table, I offered to help with the dishes.

"No, thanks. They have to be loaded in the dishwasher a certain way," said Ona Mae, as if it required great talent to pile a few dirty dishes on a rack.

I wandered into the living room, plopped down on the couch, and stared at the farm scene quilt on the wall. A house, a barn, some fields and fences.

"Does that house look familiar?" asked Martin, and I jumped.

He'd changed into an Izod shirt and shorts and running shoes, but he still had those rings on his manicured hands. "It's *this* house," he went on, sitting beside me. "When Helen and I were kids, our dad owned two hundred acres. When he sold out to a builder, Gabriel moved right up to our doorstep."

"I guess that made you sad."

"Not really. I always hated farming."

Of course. Farmers wore bib overalls and sweat-stained caps and got dirt under their fingernails.

"The gang used to razz me and call me Farmer Boy."

All at once, an idea flashed in my brain. Martin could be a gold mine of information, and I intended to pan for it. "Do you remember a guy named Woolcott from high school? Lance B. Woolcott?"

He stroked his chin and said, "Old Lanny B? Sure. Why do you ask?"

"His picture is in Mama's yearbook, and I was just curious. What was he like?"

"Big dude. Liked to talk. Good in speech and debate. Went off to a seminary after graduation." As Helen rolled her wheelchair into the living room, he said, "Sis, I think Freedom likes your farm quilt."

Smiling at me, she wheeled on past. "Martin hates it. It reminds him of slopping hogs and shoveling manure."

Martin's arm came off the back of the couch and rested lightly on my shoulder. I leaned forward a little. I wasn't used to being touched by my own mother, much less a stranger. What if he was a sick-o, like Patsy McCorkle's foster father? To get him back on track, I said, "You must have known my mother, too. Mary Margaret Avery."

"Sure, I knew her. She and Lanny B dated, matter of fact."

"Were they—? Did they—?" I felt the blood rush to my face. I couldn't flat out ask Martin if Lanny B was my father. It was too personal, and besides, how would he know anyway? "They must have made a cute couple," I said lamely.

"I guess they did."

Ona Mae swept in, rubbing lotion on her hands. "Everybody thought Lanny B and Mary Margaret would get married."

"I still can't think of him as a priest," said Martin.

"Who could?" asked Ona Mae as she disappeared down the hall. "He wasn't exactly a saint."

20

SOURPUSS AND NIT-PICKER

⭐ Ona Mae was back in a minute with a garment slung over her arm. "Marty, I'm off to the grocery store. I'll drop your suit at the cleaners."

"Tell them to watch how they hang the pants. Last time they messed up the crease."

She pecked him on the cheek and left, and he motioned to the TV and asked, "You like video games?"

"No." I'd seen kids playing at the convenience store, but it seemed like a waste of money and a mindless thing to do.

"How about movies?"

"Sometimes."

"You're not very talkative, are you?"

"I guess not."

"I'm trying to get acquainted here, and it's hard. Instead of me shooting in the dark, how about if you tell me what you like?"

"Books." Suddenly, I remembered I hadn't let Alice know we were back.

"Anything else?"

"No, just books. I've got to call my friend, Alice Murdock. Would it be all right if I use the phone?"

Martin looked puzzled or disgusted—I couldn't tell which. "Sure. There's one here and one in the kitchen. I suppose, if you want privacy, you can use the one in our bedroom."

"Which way is that?"

"Down the hall. First door on the left."

The room was beautifully decorated in teal blue, but hanging on a nail, looking totally out of place, was a pair of faded bib overalls with holes in the knees. I chuckled to myself as I dialed the phone.

"Hello?"

"Hi, Alice. It's me, Freedom."

She shrieked, and I yanked the receiver from my ear. "Freedom Jo Avery, where have you been? It's all over town that you ran away!"

I could almost see her hazel eyes smoldering. "I'm sorry," I said. "I wanted to tell you we were leaving, but I thought it'd be safer if you didn't know."

"I'm not a blabbermouth."

"I know, but Miss Harbaugh could have made it rough on you."

"She came here, to my house."

"She did?"

"Yeah. She asked where you'd gone, and she kept looking at my eyes when I said I didn't know. I guess to see if I was lying."

"So aren't you glad I didn't tell you?"

"Sort of, but I was worried about you. We hear such awful stories on the news. Where'd you go, anyway?"

"To Truman Lake. I'll tell you all about it, if you come over. I'm dying to see you."

"Over where?"

I laughed. I hadn't even thought to tell her about Martin and Ona Mae. "We're staying with the Quincys. Just a minute while I ask Martin for the address and make sure it's all right for you to come."

✦

I decided to try out my new makeup and doll myself up for Alice. When I headed back downstairs, I was enveloped by a cloud of cologne, and my lips and fingernails were a delicate rose pink.

I heard ice being clinked into glasses in the kitchen, so I went in for a drink. Theodore was mixing up some Kool-Aid, and Jackie was divvying out the ice. Martin was hovering over both of them, to see if they did it right. "That's too much sugar, son," he said.

"But the package says a cup."

"Half a cup is plenty." When Martin saw me, he said, "Kids get too much sugar. The alternative is artificial sweeteners, and they're one-way tickets to cancer."

I just looked at him, and wondered if he watched his fat intake and avoided secondhand smoke. He was turning the cookie jar, so it read "Cookies" instead of "Coo." A neatness freak. How strange that he'd keep a pair of worn-out overalls.

"Hey, Freedom," said Jackie, "Theodore plays Little League. He's gonna teach me how to pitch."

Martin laughed. "Theodore's a pretty good batter, but he couldn't hit the broad side of a barn with a beach ball."

Theodore's face turned beet red, and I did a slow burn. No dad should do that to his kid. In my book, Martin would rate a minus six. Turning my back on him, I said to Theodore, "Jackie needs all the coaching he can get. Mama promised he can play Little League next summer."

He flashed me a grateful grin. "Want some Kool-Aid?"

"I sure do. And could I have some more of that sugar? I like mine extra sweet."

Still steaming at Martin, I left the house and went out to the porch swing to wait for Alice. My temperature eased back to normal as I sipped the Kool-Aid and looked toward the tree-lined street. The sun seemed to make the sidewalk shimmer, and the smell of cut grass and heated asphalt came wafting to me on a hot breeze.

Soon a pair of long legs came into view beneath the cedar trees. I set my glass on the porch rail and went running out to meet Alice as she turned onto the sidewalk. Frizzy wisps of light brown hair were glued to her damp forehead, but she wasn't blinking every second from her contacts.

She sized me up and whistled. "I expected you to look like road kill, but you look great. What happened?"

"I discovered the sun works magic, and so do bottles and jars."

"Would magic work on your grab bag friend?"

"You don't need it," I said, linking my arm with hers. "You're already a sight for sore eyes." And she was, even though her new jungle print jump suit was so loud, I could almost hear the parrots squawk.

After only two steps, Alice stopped in her tracks and gawked at the house. "Isn't this where Laura Nell Gentry lives?"

"Yup."

"Why didn't that social worker just throw you in a meat grinder and get it over with?" Alice towed me up onto the porch, saying, "Give me a swig of that Kool-Aid. I'm dry as corn meal in a paper sack." After draining my glass, she plopped down on the swing and patted the seat beside her. "Sit. Talk. Tell me everything."

Before I could say a word, Ona Mae drove up and started unloading two bags of groceries.

I met her at the edge of the porch. "Need some help?"

"You're a little late for that. Just open the door."

After I'd done as she asked, Alice muttered, "What's her problem?"

"I don't know. I had a feeling she didn't like me the minute I walked in the door. My guess is she's putting up with us to earn some extra money. Come on, let's go upstairs." With a mischievous grin, I added, "To Laura Nell's room."

Alice rolled her eyes and followed me into the house.

Martin called to us when we were halfway up the stairs. What now? I thought, as I turned around and looked down. Is he going to inspect Alice, too?

"So you're Alice Murdock. Is your dad named Billy Joe?"

"Yes."

"Does he still have his fifty-seven Chevy?"

"Oh, yes. The Blue Babe. It's a classic. He drives it in parades."

"He was always so particular with The Babe. Wouldn't give a guy a ride if it was raining."

"He's worse now. He goes out every day and checks for fingerprints."

"Tell him Martin Quincy says hello. And if he needs more insurance on The Babe, I'm the man to see."

Alice and I went on upstairs. At the door to Laura Nell's room, she stopped and said, "Nice room. Crummy occupant. Where is the little darling?"

"Helping some second-graders at day camp."

"Bummer. They won't be happy campers."

We sat cross-legged on my bed, and Alice said, "Fill me in, starting with how you came to be roomies with Laura Nell Freak-You-Out Gentry."

When I told her, she said, "I'll bet that girl's been a real problem child. You know what I can't figure out? Why Lydia Barton runs around with her."

"Birds of a feather."

"Not really. Lydia's rich and all that, but I've never seen her do anything hateful. Not like Laura Nell."

Come to think of it, I hadn't seen Lydia mistreat anybody, either. "I just know Lydia makes me uncomfortable. I never told you this, but on the Fourth of July, I think I was wearing her Gremlins T-shirt. It came from Second Time Around, and it had a little ink blot on the shoulder, so she could have recognized it."

"Did she say anything about it?"

"No."

"Well, there you go. Laura Nell would have rubbed your nose in it, but Lydia didn't say a word. I think you're paranoid. Maybe I would be, too, if I had your plethora of problems. Oh, well, let's hear about this trip to Truman Lake."

Suppressing a smile, I ticked off on my fingers, "We ran into a Doberman, a copperhead, and some drunks. Then a tornado demolished our camp."

"Freedom Avery, give me a break. You're not Indiana Jones."

"I knew you wouldn't believe it."

"Tell me anyway. I've always liked science fiction."

"Well, the first night after we left Gabriel, nothing bad happened, but the second night, there was this vicious dog named Satan . . ."

When I was finished, Alice said, "It's a wonder you made it home all in one piece."

"I'm a survivor," I said, feeling proud.

"Let's just hope you can survive the grouch downstairs. She looks like a cat, with those green eyes and that sourpuss face."

"Martin's just as bad. Laura Nell calls him 'the inspector,' and she's right. He's a real nit-picker."

"How'd Miss Harbaugh come up with them anyway? Are they foster parents or what?"

"Not exactly. She called them a 'temporary arrangement.' "

"How long is temporary?"

"Until Mama gets home. Nineteen days."

Alice grinned. "Have you counted up the hours and the minutes?"

"Not yet."

"How's your mom's treatment going?"

"Who knows? She can't write or call until she's been there two weeks. That's this coming Monday. I can't send her a letter until then."

"Bummer. You gonna tell her about Truman Lake?"

"No way. She'd probably tear up that hospital, trying to get out. Since she's almost to the halfway point, she might as well take the whole dose."

"I guess you want me to baby-sit Bonnie's boys a couple more weeks?"

"Would you? I doubt if Ona Mae would trust me to be gone all night."

"Can't blame her. You've been a fugitive from justice," Alice said, and we collapsed in a giggling fit.

21

THE FREEDOM QUILT

★ When Alice left, I stood at the front door and watched her walk away, envying her for having a normal home to go to.

"You look lonesome."

"Oh!" I whirled around and saw Helen parked in her wheelchair. A sunbeam made her short black hair look sleek as a crow's wing.

"I didn't mean to scare you."

"That's all right. I guess I'm just a little—uh—"

"Homesick?"

"Yeah."

"Well, come with me. Maybe I can help."

I followed her down the hallway, past Martin and Ona Mae's room and into a huge, sunny bedroom.

"Excuse the mess," she said.

I stood gaping. Besides the usual furniture, there was a sewing machine, a work table, shelves piled high with fabrics, and a quilt-in-progress in a long wooden quilting frame. "Effie would love this," I said.

"Effie Waisner?" asked Helen as she situated her chair at the table.

"Yes. You know her?"

"We belong to the same quilt guild, the Piece Makers. You may have read about us: Blessed are the Piece Makers, for they create heirlooms out of scraps."

I smiled at the Biblical turn of phrase. The name fit Effie. She was a *peace*maker, too.

"Our members are rich, poor, young, old, and everything in between, but we all love starting out with a jumble of fabrics and colors and ending up with a work of art."

I touched the quilt in the frame. "This is gorgeous."

"It's almost finished. It's called Missouri Puzzle, and I made it for Ona Mae, who's hooked on jigsaw puzzles. It has thirty blocks, with sixty-five pieces in each one."

"That's almost two thousand pieces!"

"I know." Helen showed me a sketch done on graph paper of a white star in a field of red, surrounded by a border of blue. "When I heard you'd be staying with us for a while, I put my thinker to work and came up with this."

"Nice design."

"It's my version of the Lone Star quilt. I thought with a name like Freedom, the colors would be right for you."

"For me?"

"Yes, but there's a catch. You'll have to help me make it."

"I've cut a lot of quilt blocks for Effie, but I don't know much about sewing," I said. Deep down, though, I knew it would be a good way to pass the time. If I didn't have sense enough to run a dishwasher, I'd be death with a dust rag.

"I'll show you step by step. We'll use a method called strip quilting. It's speedy and it's fun." Helen laid out a ruler, some scissors, and a stack of fabrics in red, white, and blue. "We have to cut strips three inches wide, the length of the material. I'll measure while you cut."

I sat across from her and watched while she marked off a few rows on the red. I could see a resemblance between her and Martin. The fair skin, the beaked nose, the black hair. Helen's hair had no gray streaks, and I wondered if she colored hers.

She handed me the fabric, and when I started cutting, she said, "I saw your picture in the paper when you won the spelling bee. You must be one smart girl."

"I read a lot."

"I did, too, after I got polio. It was a way to escape this wheelchair and live vicariously."

Vicariously. I'd have to use that one on Alice.

"It seems like nowadays, all kids want to do is watch TV."

"We don't have one anymore. Ours broke ages ago, and we never had the money to get it fixed."

"I hope ours blows before school starts. Sitcoms and homework don't mix, and I expect there'll be war between Martin and Laura Nell."

"I gathered she's not crazy about her uncle," I said as I snipped away.

"Laura Nell's a very mixed-up girl since her dad died. I started spoiling her then—not cracking down like I should have—and it's catching up with me now. She needs an authority figure, and Martin fills the bill."

"My ears are burning," said Martin from the doorway. "Somebody's talking about me."

"Hi," said Helen. "Come on in."

He ambled in and sat on the edge of the bed. "Sis, you really ought to put up a sign that says 'Disaster Area.' This room gets more cluttered by the day."

"It's organized clutter. I know where to find every pattern, every swatch of fabric, every spool of thread."

"If you say so." Martin motioned to the strip in my hand. "I see my sis sold you on the Freedom quilt. When she gets through with you, you'll be seeing quilt blocks in your sleep."

The Freedom quilt. I rolled the words around in my mind. A nice name, if only it hadn't come from Martin.

He stayed a few minutes longer, making small talk, with me wishing all the while that he would leave. I couldn't forget how he'd embarrassed Theodore over the pitching, and I had the weirdest feeling he was inspecting me.

When we were alone again, I asked Helen, "Is Laura Nell interested in quilting?"

"Not yet, but maybe someday. It runs in the family. My mother and grandmother made quilts. See over there on the trunk?"

I glanced at the faded quilts, one in jewel colors and the other in shades of brown.

"Mother made the Jewelry Box. Grandma made the Log Cabin."

"That would be great, to have something your grandmother made. I never had a grandmother."

"You feel cheated, huh?"

I almost dropped the scissors. Helen knew exactly how I felt. "Mama's folks were killed in a fire, and she won't tell me who my father is."

"I'm sure she has her reasons."

"Did you know Mama?"

"Vaguely. I was a couple of years older. I knew about the fire and that she started drinking. But now that she's making the long, hard climb back to sobriety, she's bound to feel better about herself. Maybe she'll see things from a different perspective and stop dwelling on the past." Helen's gaze traveled to the dresser, to a photograph of herself and a smiling young man.

"Your husband?" I asked softly.

She nodded. "I used to feel ugly and deformed, but Larry made me feel beautiful. When he died, it took a long time for me to pull myself together. It was my father who helped me put things in perspective."

"How?"

"He always felt guilty that I had gotten polio. While trying to convince him that the past was gone and he couldn't change it, I learned the same lesson myself."

"How'd you get it? Polio, I mean."

"Daddy was afraid of vaccinations, because he almost died from the typhoid one they gave him in the service. When the school insisted that Martin and I had to have our shots, Daddy went up there and raised a ruckus. No shots."

"How come you got polio and Martin didn't?"

"Same reason some people are allergic to penicillin and some aren't."

"Hi, Mom," said Laura Nell as she whisked into the room. Casting me a drop-dead glance, she kissed the top of her mother's head.

"Hi, hon. How was day camp?"

"OK. I showed the kids how to sew on a button. They ate it up. Monday we're going to poach an egg." She fingered the strips piled up on the table. "Are you two going to hole up in here and quilt all the time?"

"Of course not. And you're welcome to join us anytime you want."

"No, thanks, I'll leave the quilting to you and Betsy Ross."

✦

During supper, Ona Mae announced, "Tomorrow I'm taking Freedom and Jackie shopping."

I choked on my cole slaw. "Us?"

"Yes. Your clothes are a disgrace."

A *disgrace?* She's just worried about what other people will think, I fumed. And what right does she have to go snooping in our closets?

Ona Mae drummed her nails on the table, thinking. "We'll pick up shorts and shirts and tennis shoes, and something nice for church."

"I've got a nice dress," I said.

"That pink one I saw? It's more for a special occasion, not church."

"She wore it to the awards ceremony," said Jackie.

"Awards ceremony?" echoed Martin. "What award?"

"I was named top student in seventh grade."

"Big deal," said Laura Nell. "You beat Lydia Barton by a fraction of a percentage point."

"Ah, the green eye of jealousy," said Martin.

"I'm not jealous."

Ignoring his niece, Martin turned to Helen and asked, "Would Lydia be Sid and Dorothy's daughter?"

"Yes."

"I ran into Sid the other day. That old rascal owns the Ford dealership."

Ford dealership. No wonder Lydia could afford Pepsi by the case.

✦

Ages had passed since morning and Truman Lake. I needed some time to myself, but unless I wanted to spend the whole evening on the toilet, there was no private place for me to go. Laura Nell was in her room, and Martin, Jackie, and Theodore had taken over the living room. Ona Mae and Helen were working on that puzzle in the dining room. I retreated to the kitchen with a *Reader's Digest*.

After a while, the women gave up on the puzzle, and I heard Martin tell Theodore to quit playing video games and go memorize his lines.

Jackie, looking lonesome, came into the kitchen and asked if he could have some cookies.

I held the cookie jar for him, and when I put it back, I deliberately turned it to read "Coo." "Why such a long face, Cotton Top?"

"Tomorrow's Saturday. We'll miss our cinnamon rolls." He broke open an Oreo, licked off the icing, then told me good-night and left the kitchen.

I watched him go, thinking how his heart and his stomach operated on the same wavelength. To him, cinnamon rolls represented Mama.

I read a couple of stories in the *Digest,* and I heard the news begin on TV. My eyelids were growing so heavy, they kept closing all by themselves, but I put off going upstairs. I wasn't up to being insulted by Laura Nell.

"Somebody's asleep at the switch," said Martin, patting my hand and jarring me to attention. "Care to join me for a bedtime snack?"

I moved my hand away. He was too touchy-touchy for me. "No, thanks." I waited to see if he would reposition the cookie jar. When he did, I said, "I'm going up to bed."

"Long day, huh?"

"Eternity." I left the kitchen and passed through the living room, where Ona Mae was staring at the tube. "Good night."

" 'Night," she replied, without looking at me.

To my everlasting relief, Laura Nell was in the bathroom, and I didn't even mind that I couldn't brush my teeth. I changed into my nightgown, then turned down the covers on the bed, smiling at the thought of the Freedom quilt. I crawled between the sheets and switched off the light. Running my hand back and forth beneath the mattress, I breathed the scent of clean sheets and laundry soap and fell asleep thinking about Mama.

I dreamed she and I were talking on Effie's porch swing, and she was about to reveal the secret of my father. All at once, the swinging became violent, and we were sucked up into a tornado and bombarded with trash and minnow buckets. A copperhead got twisted around my ankle, and I screamed.

"Hey, Freedom, cool it," someone said.

I propped myself up on one elbow and blinked against the light. There stood a girl with puffball hair and green pajamas, demanding to know if this went on every night.

"No. Sorry," I muttered. I rolled over and pulled the covers up to my ears. It was one of life's cruel tricks—waking up from a nightmare and finding myself face to face with Laura Nell Gentry.

22

SWEATING THE SMALL STUFF

★ I woke up grumpy Saturday morning, and seeing Laura Nell asleep in the next bed didn't help. I snatched a disgraceful shirt off a hanger and disgraceful shorts from a drawer, and dressed myself before clumping down the stairs, disgracefully.

Halfway down, I saw Martin snoozing on the couch. A coffee mug sat beside him on the floor, and a section of the newspaper lay open on his chest. He was dressed for the office, no doubt in a suit that wouldn't wrinkle.

In the kitchen, Ona Mae sat drinking coffee and checking the ads in *The Gazette*. Her auburn hair was styled in soft curls, and her blue-green eye shadow matched the flowers in her sundress. She looked nice, but I wouldn't tell her. I just said, "Hi."

"Hi. I'm glad you're up. I want to talk to you."

She probably knew I'd gone to bed without brushing my teeth. Was that another disgrace?

"There's orange juice in the refrigerator," she said, eyes still on the paper.

After taking a glass from the cabinet, I turned the

cookie jar to "Coo." Then I poured the juice, sat down, and stared at the red and white checks in the tablecloth.

"Why'd you run away from Gabriel?"

"Huh?"

"Why'd you run away?"

"Oh—uh—I— After Mama left, we were going to be sent to the juvenile justice center or separate foster homes. I didn't like the choices."

"Choices are a part of life. Some are good. Some aren't. We have to consider the consequences. The choice you made was dangerous."

I traced my finger over some checks on the table-cloth.

"Running away never solves anything. It didn't help you, did it?"

I traced more checks.

"Did it?" she persisted.

"I guess not."

"Of course, I realize you probably haven't had the best guidance. Your mother being an alcoholic. Not knowing who your father is."

I glared at her. Did she mean that I didn't know who my father was? Or was she insinuating that Mama had been with lots of men and didn't know which one had planted me? "Mama does OK with Jackie and me," I said, keeping my voice level. "It's not her fault we ran away."

"But it *is* her fault for putting you in that position in the first place."

Just who was Ona Mae Quincy to be passing judgment? "You don't know what you're talking about," I said. "You don't know anything about us."

"I know all I need to know." Ona Mae got up, yanked an apron from the drawer, and tied it around her waist.

"Got any more of that witch's brew?" asked Martin, standing in the doorway with his mug.

"Just who are you calling a witch?" she snapped.

"Whoa, now, Mother," he said as he went over and straightened the cookie jar. "I meant the coffee. It's strong enough to walk by itself."

✦

Ona Mae had cooled off by the time she'd finished cooking breakfast. She tried to make friendly conversation, but it didn't work with me. I didn't say one word as I ate my sausage, eggs, and toast.

When Ona Mae asked who wanted to go shopping with us, Laura Nell said, "Not me. I think I'll stay home and bake *cookies*."

"How about you, Helen? We're going to Mighty Mart."

"No, I don't need anything, and having me along would slow you down."

"Hey, it's Saturday. We've got all day. You're welcome to come."

"No, thanks. Maybe I'll help Laura Nell with the cookies."

Laura Nell frowned, and I knew she hadn't planned to do any baking.

"I'll take Freedom and Jackie, of course, and Theodore. . . . Now, son, don't give me that look. You need new tennis shoes. After we've shopped for you and Jackie, you boys can pick up a hamburger at Hardee's and go on to the ball game."

"What time is your game?" asked Martin.

"One o'clock," said Theodore.

"I'll be able to make it, since the office closes at noon. When's your next play practice?"

"Tonight at seven."

"Have you learned your lines yet?"

"Well—"

"Look, son, everyone's counting on you to be King Herod. Are you up to it or not?"

"Relax, Martin," said Helen. "They've still got two weeks."

"Yeah, don't sweat the small stuff," said Laura Nell. "I'll help him myself before practice."

Martin frowned at her. "I hardly think the play is 'small stuff.' There'll be hundreds of people at that celebration."

"May I be excused?" asked Theodore.

"You've barely touched your breakfast," said Ona Mae.

"Leave the boy alone, Mother," said Martin. "He's smart enough to know if he's hungry or not."

✦

When we reached Mighty Mart, I told myself not to sweat the small stuff. If the Quincys wanted to blow money on temporary kids, that was their problem. The store was big and bright and airy, and I spent a long time in the dressing room, trying to make up my mind. Every shirt was soft as a cotton ball and had the chemical smell of new fabric, instead of the taint of other people's sweat.

I finally settled on three pullovers—a plain light blue, a striped one in red and white, and a white one with gold buttons and two big pockets. All three shirts would look good with the new denim skirt and the two pairs of walking shorts that had pleats down the front. I gathered up my selections and took them to Ona Mae.

Right away, she steered me to the underwear and told me to pick out some bras and panties.

"I don't need them," I said.

"Yes, you do. Yours are ragged."

"What difference does that make? No one's going to see them."

"Martin's orders."

"Does he have a dress code or something?"

"Don't be a smart aleck. He told me to outfit you kids from the skin out."

✦

Laura Nell, Helen, and Martin were eating lunch when we got home. A plate of cookies sat on the counter. Laura Nell had had to carry through.

"I made ham sandwiches for you," said Helen. "They're in the fridge."

When I finished mine, Martin said, "I've still got a few minutes before the ball game. How about showing me what you bought?"

I set my bags on the end of the table and displayed one garment at a time, being careful not to drag out the underwear. Before I knew what she was doing, Laura Nell pulled out a lacy bra and said, "Hmmm, sexy."

Everyone laughed, and I felt my face go hot and red as I snatched the bra from her and crammed it back in the sack.

I fled upstairs to her room and closed the door hard, but as I folded the shorts and hung up the shirts and the skirt, my embarrassment ebbed away. This fall, I wouldn't look like a sparrow in a school full of robins.

I put on the striped shirt and navy shorts with new bobby socks and tennies. I was leaning toward the mirror, applying fresh lipstick, when the floor creaked in the hall two seconds before Laura Nell burst into the room.

"Haven't you ever heard of knocking?" I said.

"Why should I? It's my room. I'm supposed to tell you to give my mom thirty minutes for a nap, and then go down and work on the quilt." Her gaze swept over me, top to bottom. "Red, white, and blue. You must really think you're Betsy Ross." She pulled a magazine from the night stand and plopped down on the bed.

I knew I'd eventually think of a dozen things I should have said, but for now my mind was blank. Unable to baffle her with my wit, I made a fast exit instead.

On my way downstairs, I heard Martin calling to Ona Mae, who was in the living room, "Those keys have to be here someplace."

"I didn't touch them," she said. "Don't expect me to keep track of your things. I've already got more than I can handle. Two extra kids, and that Freedom has a mouth on her that won't—" She stopped speaking as her green eyes locked with mine.

"Here they are," said Martin, coming into the room. "They were under your purse on the cabinet." His eyes got big when he saw me, and he stuffed the keys in his shorts pocket. "Well, what have we here?" He came to me, put both hands on my shoulders, and turned me around slowly. "Those clothes you picked out are real pretty. You'll be breaking boys' hearts before long."

Ona Mae stiffened, reminding me of a cat arching its back.

I pulled away from Martin and went out to the porch swing. These Quincys were weird. Ona Mae was a certified grouch, and Martin was a flirt.

✦

"One cutting hand, raring to go," I said, snipping the air with my fingers.

"Good," chuckled Helen. "We'll finish cutting today and be ready to start sewing Monday."

"Why not tomorrow?"

"Church in the morning. Guild in the afternoon. Want to go?"

I thought of Effie, how her wrinkled face would light up when she found out I was making a whole quilt from scratch. "OK."

It was good to be alone with Helen, to feel so much

at ease. We marked and cut and talked about a dozen different things. I even opened up about Mama's drinking, and about how she'd once let Jackie go to the park and forgotten where he was. "I was all set to call the police," I said, "when he came walking in the door."

"It's tough sometimes, being a big sister. You feel so responsible, so protective. Until this happened," Helen said, motioning to her legs, "I was always taking the blame for something Martin did, just to keep him out of trouble. Now the shoe is on the other foot. He feels responsible for me, and protective."

The way I saw it, he felt responsible for keeping the whole world in shape. "He's been nice enough to me, but I don't think he's very fair with Theodore. He seems so—so critical."

"He is, and yet he loves that boy dearly. Martin's fighting a battle right now. With himself. He and Daddy never did see eye to eye, and he waited too long to make things right. After the funeral, he latched onto a pair of Daddy's overalls. It's like picking at a scab. He has a wound that doesn't heal."

✦

I was in the kitchen, helping Laura Nell set the table for supper, when Martin and the boys came home from the ball game. Ona Mae asked who won.

"They did," mumbled Theodore.

"You gave it to them," said Martin. He looked at Ona Mae. "Three runs. The boy stands in right field, daydreaming I guess, and misses a fly ball."

"I thought Ricky was gonna get it," said Theodore.

"Ricky? He plays center field."

"He always catches the flies."

"Somebody has to. You're afraid of the ball."

Theodore ears turned red, and his eyes glistened with tears. He left the room in a hurry, but Laura Nell said, "What's the big deal? It's just a ball game."

"That's right, Martin," said Ona Mae. "I don't see—"

"He didn't try, Mother. He didn't even try."

✦

Laura Nell helped Theodore with his lines before play practice. I was in her room and both doors were open, so I could hear her coaching him across the hall. She was patient—I'll give her that. Every time Theodore had a part, she had to tell him the first few words. Was he incapable of memorizing, I wondered, or did he just have a mental block?

Pretty soon, Ona Mae came upstairs and asked, "How's it going?"

"Not good, Mom," said Theodore. "I'll never get this."

"Don't let your father hear you say that."

"If he thinks this play's so important, why doesn't he learn the part? Then I wouldn't be up in front of everybody, looking dumb."

"You're not dumb. Don't say that."

"Tell you what," said Laura Nell. "When we get to the church, don't think about Uncle Martin. Don't

think about the crowd. Just pretend it's you and me and nobody else."

"If I could pretend that, I'd be the world's greatest actor."

"You've got it, cuz. Think positive."

✦

Jackie and I went along when Martin took the kids to play practice. I didn't especially want to go anywhere with the inspector, but I didn't want the third degree again from Ona Mae, either.

Up the street in the subdivision, Martin slowed down to let a car pull out of a driveway. He waved, and the driver waved back. I didn't know the woman, but I recognized the girl in the passenger seat. Lydia Barton. I might have known she'd live in this neighborhood.

Out of the blue, Martin said, "She who dies with the most fabric wins."

Puzzled, I looked at Laura Nell.

She crossed her eyes and whirled a finger near her temple.

"I'm not crazy," said Martin, eyeing her in the rearview mirror. "I was reading Dorothy's bumper sticker. She's quilt crazy, like your mother."

Laura Nell didn't crack a smile.

At the church, when Theodore opened the car door, Martin said, "Break a leg, son."

"Break a leg?" echoed Jackie.

Martin tousled his cottony hair. "That's how you wish an actor good luck."

Laura Nell announced to no one in particular, "Break a leg is what he'll do to Theodore if he doesn't get this right," then got out and slammed the door.

I watched her go into the church. She had a way of getting under my skin, and yet I no longer saw her as a complete jerk.

Martin drove Jackie and me around Gabriel, showing us where he'd roamed as a kid. When we passed a water tower that sprouted from a field like a giant inverted onion, he said, "My buddies and I scouted for many an Indian here, back when this was all woods."

I wondered if he'd ever told Theodore that.

The tour ended with Martin pulling into the parking lot of a rundown restaurant called "Ida's Cafe." He asked, "Anybody game for some sarsaparilla?"

"Sassa-what?" I said, and Jackie snorted.

"Girls don't know anything. Sarsaparilla. It's what the good cowboys drank in the old West."

"It's a fancy name for strawberry pop," chuckled Martin.

The smell of roast beef and gravy greeted us as we entered the dim cafe. It was empty—no customers, and not even a waitress that I could see.

"They saved us the best seat in the house," said Martin, taking my arm and guiding me to a well-worn plastic booth. Jackie and I sat on opposite sides of the table, while Martin went over to play the jukebox. Elvis Presley began crooning "Love Me Tender" as Martin slid into the booth beside me. His spicy aftershave didn't mix well with beef gravy.

A woman with brassy yellow hair and gobs of makeup pushed through some swinging doors from the kitchen. "Sorry. Didn't hear you come in."

"Ida, you always did say me and my gang had a way of sneaking up on you."

Ida tilted her head and peered at him. "Marty? Is that you?"

"The one and only."

"It's been years. Are you back here visiting?"

"Nope. Ona Mae and I moved here in May. We're staying with Helen in the folks' old place."

"Ona Mae? I thought—"

"Married her after Uncle Sam sent me to Germany. We've got one son, who's over at the church."

"Then whose kids are these?"

"They're—uh—friends of ours. That's Jackie, and this is his sister, Freedom." Martin slipped an arm across my shoulders. "They want to try some of your famous sarsaparilla."

"Coming right up," said Ida, leaving to get our drinks.

I suddenly realized how much I disliked Martin Quincy. Two whole months in Gabriel, and he hadn't treated Theodore to a sarsaparilla. Well, he was in for it now. I was going to turn that cookie jar every chance I got.

23
THE PIECE MAKERS

★ The next morning, I wanted to go to my own church. No such luck. Martin insisted we all worship together.

Laura Nell was supposed to take me to our Sunday school class, but when I stopped to use the rest room, she disappeared. I found the class by myself, and as soon as I stepped in the door, I knew I was in enemy territory. There sat Laura Nell, Sally Sumners, and Lydia Barton, flirting with four boys from school.

Everybody stopped talking to stare holes through me and my new blue shirt and skirt. My face was all but sizzling.

"Freedom," said Lydia, finally. "There's a seat over here by me."

I painted on a smile and forced myself to walk into the room and sit beside her. As usual, she looked like a million dollars with that cute pug nose and short, dark, feathery hair. Her skirt was brilliant white against her bright red summer sweater.

"Where've you been hiding out?" asked Steven Blake, looking me up and down.

I narrowed my eyes at him. Was that a crack about my running away, or was he just making conversation?

"I haven't seen you since the spelling bee," said Lydia. "You look . . . different. Really sharp."

"Thanks," I mumbled. At least I knew *this* shirt wasn't hers.

"Congratulations on winning the trophy," said Sally. "That was a nice picture of you in the paper. I was away at camp, but my mom saved it for me."

"What paper?" asked Steven. "I didn't see it."

"You can't read anyway."

"Joe Richie, you're such a dolt," said Lydia. To me, she said, "I hear you're staying at Laura Nell's."

I shot a glance at Laura Nell, but she was making eyes at Brandon Willis. I hoped she hadn't blabbed about the treatment center. "Yes, I— My brother and I'll be there while our mother's in the hospital. It's only temporary."

"I hope your mom's OK," said Lydia.

The teacher came in then, apologizing for being late.

During the lesson, I looked at my hands, at the nail polish gleaming rose pink in the sunlight. I traced the curve of my pinkies. What was different about the kids in this room? They'd hardly noticed me at school. Now all of a sudden I was the center of attention. Had they changed, or had I?

Could I have been wrong about my classmates? Was I paranoid, as Alice said? Guiltily, I thought about the few times, early on, when kids at school had tried to talk to me. I'd clammed up because I knew

Laura Nell had spread the word about Mama's drinking. Maybe I'd been a snob. That idea struck me as hilarious. Freedom Avery, the grab bag snob.

After class, Lydia caught me in the hall. "I think Steven likes you. He kept sneaking glances during the lesson."

I was flabbergasted. Lydia Barton, the girl with a plethora of Pepsi, was being chummy with *me*.

"Where do you plan to sit during worship service?"

"I don't know."

"Well, then, come with me. A bunch of us always go up in the balcony at the back of the church."

From the balcony, I could see Helen in her wheelchair in the aisle, next to Martin in a pew. He had his arm around Ona Mae, and every once in a while, he'd lean forward and look down his row, checking to see if Theodore and Jackie were behaving themselves. Inspecting them in church.

The kids I was with were surprisingly quiet, maybe because their parents could turn around and give them the evil eye if they caused a commotion. Joe snapped Steven once with a rubber band, and Laura Nell and Sally wrote notes back and forth. Other than that, there were no disturbances. Martin had no reason to turn around and inspect me.

✦

"How'd you like our church?" asked Martin as he spread butter on a hot roll.

"I liked it fine," I said, and meant it. "Everyone was real neighborly."

"That's the idea. They teach us to be our brother's

keeper," said Laura Nell, ogling my blue shirt and khaki shorts to remind me that her uncle had paid for them.

When dinner was over, Helen said to her, "I sure wish you'd go with Freedom and me to the guild meeting."

"Not a chance. Too many old ladies."

"All right then. I hate to eat and run, but I'd like to get there early, since I have to use the back door." Helen had spoken matter-of-factly, but I sensed she was self-conscious about the wheelchair.

"Need a ride?" asked Martin.

"No, it's just down the street at the Bartons'."

Lydia's house. A few hours ago, I would have avoided it like the plague.

Helen fetched her Missouri Puzzle quilt, and we left. When we reached the Bartons' house, we cut across the driveway and went out back to the patio.

The woman I'd seen driving Lydia opened a sliding glass door.

"Hi, Dorothy," said Helen. "I brought Freedom Avery, a new quilter."

"Are you keeping her in stitches?" asked Dorothy, and we all laughed.

Like Lydia, Dorothy had short dark hair and a smooth complexion, but I was surprised at the way she was dressed—a Royals T-shirt, blue jeans, and scuffed sandals.

Inside, I was momentarily blinded by the sun, but when a familiar voice said, "Freedom, child, what brings you here?" I grinned at Effie's lumpy silhouette.

My eyes adjusted, and I saw she was all gussied up in a flowered dress and loafers that were murder on her corns.

"Freedom's working on a Lone Star quilt," said Helen.

"Well, don't that make this old heart proud! Like they say, if I'd known you were coming, I'd have baked a cake."

"Cake we don't need," said Dorothy, patting her hips. "Your vegetable tray is just fine. Why don't you girls go on into the living room? You can help Janis and Vicki answer the door."

Helen left the kitchen, but Effie stopped me, saying, "I want to hear more about this quilt."

I pulled up a stool and filled her in, while she minced some green onions into sour cream, and Dorothy poured ingredients for punch into a crystal bowl. I was watching the fizz of ginger ale, when Dorothy said, "You're a very pretty girl, but you don't look like your mother."

My head snapped up. "You know Mama?"

"We were best friends, off and on, through high school."

"Off and on? I thought best friends were best friends, no matter what."

"Not with Mary Margaret. She changed with the weather. There were six of us who hung around together. Lanny B and Mary Margaret, Sid and me, and Marty Q and Wynona. You probably know them as Martin and Ona Mae."

From the note in Mama's yearbook, I'd assumed

Marty Q was a girl! Thinking out loud, I said, "Martin was with Mama when she threw Lanny's ring into the Lake of the Ozarks."

"I don't know. She wasn't speaking to me at the time."

"Tell me about her and Lanny B."

Dorothy twisted the cap off another bottle. "Cute couple, but never really suited to each other."

"No wonder," said Effie. "He was Catholic, and she was a hard-shelled Baptist."

"Mama?" No way. She'd always seen to it that Jackie and I went to Sunday school, but she wouldn't set foot in the church herself.

Dorothy glanced at Effie, as if deciding what or how much to say. "After Mary Margaret's folks died, Lanny B started pressuring her to join the Catholic Church and marry him. She quit going to church altogether. She was mad at Lanny and God and everybody else."

"And pregnant with me."

Effie's teeth clacked. "Such language, child. In my day, it was called 'in the family way.' "

"We called it 'in trouble,' " said Dorothy with a nervous laugh.

I glanced from one to the other. They were uncomfortable just talking about pregnancy. How hard it must have been for Mama, being pregnant with me.

"I'm not sure just when Mary Margaret got—uh—in trouble," Dorothy went on, "but I know she was a different person after the fire."

"Who wouldn't be?" said Effie.

"We'd gone to a party after graduation, or she might have burned to death, too."

"I—I didn't know it happened on graduation night," I said in a strangled voice.

Effie nodded solemnly. "I always thought the flames killed more than your mama's folks. They destroyed her dreams for the future, too."

"And Lanny's," said Dorothy. "He wanted to settle down, have a family. When it didn't work out for him and Mary Margaret, he went off to the seminary, and she—"

"—took up drinking," finished Effie. "I talked to that child till I was hoarse."

"We all did. The only person she would halfway listen to was Marty, and that was because he and Wynona—Ona Mae—had broken up, and he was as lost as she was."

A cackling sound erupted from the living room. "Effie," I said, "those women in there, did they know Mama back then?"

"Some did, but if you're worrying about gossip, don't. I told them a long time ago not to be judging Mary Margaret until they've walked a mile in her shoes."

✦

Quilts were being unfolded and admired—Missouri Puzzle, Turkey Tracks, Triple Irish Chain. Though I was sharing a love seat with Effie, I felt detached, isolated from the crowd. I was piecing parts of Mama's life together. Let them piece the quilts.

A lady gave a demonstration on pivot points, what-ever they were. Every once in a while, the women would burst out laughing. I'd fake hysteria at the appropriate times, then go back to my own private thoughts.

When it came time for refreshments, the conversa-tion turned to calico and poly-cotton blends. I slipped out to the patio to eat by myself in a lawn chair.

I was nibbling a tiny sandwich when the sliding glass door opened, bells jingled, and something long and white and furry scurried onto my ankles. I shrieked and almost dropped my plate.

"Easy, Ferdinand," said Lydia, pulling on his leash.

"What is that?" I gasped.

"A ferret. He's an albino. All white, see, with shocking pink eyes. Mom says he looks like a rat."

He did, sort of, but I couldn't say that. I was speechless, in fact. Ferrets were related to weasels and polecats, and here stood Lydia Barton with one, just as calm as you please.

"Watch your plate," said Lydia as Ferdinand started climbing my leg. "He'll run you over for an olive." She sat down and pulled him onto her lap.

I finally found my voice, but I didn't want to talk about the ferret, so I said, "Your mom went to school with my mom."

"I know. I started to say something to you once, but you got this wild look on your face and ran into the bathroom."

It all came back. Lydia had asked, "Is your mother's name Mary Margaret?" and I'd thought she was going to bring up the Girl Scout cookies. "I'm sorry. I guess I've been sort of standoffish since I came here."

"I can see why, after Laura Nell opened her big mouth. As if she had anything to crow about. She's been caught shoplifting twice. The first time, she got a slap on the hand. The second time, the judge sentenced her to community service. That's why she's helping at day camp."

I tried to feel smug about Laura Nell's shoplifting, but I couldn't—not when I remembered how she'd stood up for Theodore.

✦

I wanted to ask Martin about the ring and the Lake of the Ozarks, but he never got far enough away from Ona Mae. Once, when I thought he was by himself in the kitchen, I went after him, only to back right out again when I found him kissing her like a dying man sucking air.

After supper, I went up to Laura Nell's room. The floor squeaked, and she glanced up as I tapped on the door frame. She was on her bed, listening to the radio and painting her toenails.

"Can we call a truce or something?" I said. "They're watching a *Star Trek* movie downstairs, and I can't stand all that space jargon."

"Just stay on your side, and don't bother my stuff."

Interesting comment, since she was using my nail polish. "I won't bother you at all. I'll be writing a letter to Mama." I arranged my pillows and curled up

on the bed to write, using paper and pen I'd borrowed
from Helen. Composing the letter was almost as hard
as trying to talk to Mama, and it took a long time. I'd
write a sentence or two and then have to stop and
think for a few minutes. Finally, I finished and read it
to myself:

> *Dear Mama:*
>
> *Jackie and I've been missing you a lot.
> When you left, we walked several miles every
> day. He fell on a rock and hurt his leg, but he'll
> be good as new Tuesday when the stitches
> come out.*
>
> *We're staying with Martin and Ona Mae
> Quincy and their son Theodore in Gabriel.
> The Quincys live with his sister, who's in a
> wheelchair, and her daughter, who's in my
> class at school.*
>
> *Jackie likes Theodore and follows him ev-
> erywhere. Theodore's going to teach him how
> to pitch.*
>
> *Martin said he remembers you from high
> school. Ona Mae isn't very friendly, so I don't
> talk to her unless I have to. Helen (Martin's
> sister) is nice, though, and she gave me the
> paper and stamp for this letter. She's helping
> me make a quilt in red, white, and blue. She
> said since my name is Freedom, the colors
> seemed right for me.*
>
> *I saw Effie today at a guild meeting. I met
> one of your old friends, too—Dorothy Barton.*

Her daughter is Lydia Barton, the girl I'm always trying to beat in school. I thought Lydia was a snob, but I was wrong. Snobs don't keep ferrets in their rooms.

How's it going at the treatment center? I'll bet not having to work every day makes it seem like a vacation.

Mama, I don't want to make you mad, but I really need to know who my father is. Now that you're not drinking, maybe you can see it from my side. I wouldn't want to live with him or anything, so you don't have to worry about that. He might not claim me anyway, because I'm gonky and I have this honker of a nose (ha ha). I know it's hard for you to talk about, but can't you just tell me in a letter?

Please write soon. We miss you.

Love, Freedom
XOXOXOXO

24

DIGGING UP THE DIRT

★ Monday morning, the house was quiet, with Martin gone to work, Laura Nell and Helen at aquatic therapy, and Jackie and Theodore out playing ball. As I was coming in from mailing Mama's letter, Ona Mae asked me to gather up everybody's dirty clothes and take them to the laundry room.

I did as she asked, then went into the living room and called Alice. When I told her about the "Coo" on the cookie jar, I thought she'd bust a gut laughing.

"You're incredible," she whooped.

"Just a little trick I pulled out of my grab bag."

"So what else have you been up to?"

"I'm working on a quilt. It's red, white, and blue. A Freedom quilt."

"Sounds like a riot."

"Helen took me to her guild meeting yesterday at Lydia Barton's house."

"No kidding."

"I talked to Lydia for a while. She's got a ferret named Ferdinand that sleeps with her and messes on the floor and goes bonkers over olives."

"You're pulling my leg."

"No, honest. She wants to be a zoologist. I told her we'd live our lives more vicariously—me as a librarian and you as a writer. She remembers all those stories you wrote in Mrs. Rodenbeck's class, and she thinks you definitely have talent."

"See, I told you that girl was all right. Uh-oh, hold the phone. Tina the terrible is fixing to dump a whole gallon of milk." Alice laid down the receiver and went to see about Tina. When she came back on the line, she said, "Mom's working this morning, so yours truly has to run the vacuum and baby-sit. What's on your schedule for the day? Another get-together with Lydia?"

I heard a hint of jealousy, but I didn't let on. "I'm going to start sewing my quilt."

"Whatever turns your crank. How about you and Laura Nell? Has she made threats against your life?"

"She's not so bad, really. She sticks up for Theodore when his dad gets on his case. Which is just about every time the poor kid turns around." A noise called my attention to the doorway, and there stood Ona Mae, looking mad enough to split boulders with a glance. "Look, Alice, I've got to go. I'll catch you later. 'Bye." Carefully, I set the receiver in its cradle, then skulked toward the stairs.

"Hold it right there."

In slow motion, I turned to face Ona Mae.

"What goes on in this house is nobody's business. I don't appreciate you discussing my son with outsiders or telling people that Martin's a tyrant."

"I—I—"

The cat eyes blazed at me. "You don't know the first thing about Martin or the problems he's had, little missy, so don't be shooting off your mouth. As for Theodore, he'll make it just fine without your interference."

Ona Mae stalked off to the laundry room, and I knew that from here on out, I'd bend over backwards to stay out of her way.

✦

At the door of Helen's bedroom, I saluted and said, "Freedom Avery reporting for duty."

Helen rolled away from the sewing machine. "It's all yours."

"I've never used one before."

"It's not that hard. Put the fabric under here, turn the wheel, then press this gadget with your knee. Go ahead and practice on these scraps."

When I could sew a straight seam, I stitched together the first batch of quilt strips. "They don't look like much," I said, holding up the strip of red, white, and red.

"Don't worry. There's a method to this madness." When Helen cut the swatch into diagonal strips, they became rows of white diamonds with eight red diamonds at each end.

I sewed those strips together, and I had a big white star surrounded by red. "I know I sound like Jackie," I said, "but this is neat."

"It is, isn't it?" Helen said, sounding pleased.

"Mama'll be impressed . . . I hope."

"Of course she will. I think you'll find that your mother's a different person when she leaves the treatment center. My father was."

"Your father was a drinker?"

"Not just a drinker. A drunk."

My mouth fell open. Coming from Helen, the word "drunk" was unexpected.

Helen didn't notice. Her thoughts were miles away. "Martin and I grew up in this house, tiptoeing around, afraid to breathe, never knowing if Daddy would come home slap-happy-cheerful or roaring drunk and mean."

And I'd thought I had it rough with Mama.

"I woke up one night and heard him downstairs, yelling. I got up and found Martin crying at the foot of the stairs, and Daddy choking Mother with his belt. Martin had Daddy's twenty-two with the hammer pulled back, ready to fire. When I yelled for him not to shoot, Daddy grabbed the rifle."

I tried to imagine Martin as that little boy, but I couldn't. "Did your dad ever hurt you kids?"

"If you mean physically, no, because he had Mother to bully. But he abused us verbally. Shaming Martin for wetting the bed, me for being a tomboy. Verbal abuse beats you down. It hurts much worse than a slap across the mouth."

I'd gotten smacked a few times by Mama, but she'd never cut me down with words. Just the opposite, in fact. I could almost hear her saying I was going to be Somebody Someday.

"One thing about Daddy—he was good at remorse. After he'd been especially mean, he'd try to make it up to us. Sometimes he'd take us fishing, or he'd buy us gum and candy bars. After I got polio, he couldn't do enough for me. Lavished me with presents we couldn't afford. He even cut down on his drinking for a while, although that didn't last. It got even worse after Mother died. I was married by then, but Martin was a senior in high school."

"When did your dad finally stop?"

"Five years ago. He went to the same treatment center where your mother is now. He got dried out and became the kind of father I needed, because by then, Larry had cancer. After a year or so, Daddy started selling off the farm, bit by bit. He hadn't told me he had liver damage, so I thought he was just slowing down." A tear rolled down Helen's cheek and plopped onto her lap quilt. "After he died, I found out he'd been paying off Larry's hospital bills. It hit Martin pretty hard that he'd never made his peace with Daddy."

Later, I called Alice and brought her up to date.

"Well, that explains why Martin's such a pain," she said. "He's a classic example of the adult child of an alcoholic. Remember that report I did? Wait a minute, and I'll dig up the dirt." Alice left the phone, and when she came back, she recited, "Doesn't know what 'normal' is. Has low self-esteem. Has problems with intimate relationships. Doesn't allow himself to have fun. Super responsible."

"That sounds like Martin, all right, except for the

low self-esteem. But Helen had the same background, and she doesn't have those symptoms."

"Different strokes for different folks. Martin's definitely not normal. How many people do you know who worry about the 'Coo' on a cookie jar?"

"None. And you know what else? He keeps a pair of his dad's old overalls hanging in his room. To punish himself, I guess."

"Your honor, I rest my case."

25

THE INSPECTOR GENERAL

On Tuesday, Jackie got his stitches out.

I was expecting a letter from Mama, but it didn't come, either that day or the next.

I spent my time turning the cookie jar when no one was looking and working on my quilt. When I finished sewing the strips together Thursday morning, I spread out the quilt top on Helen's bed. The big white star in the center seemed to twinkle—until I saw a glaring mistake in the border. In the field of red was a blue diamond, and in the field of red, a blue. "Oh, Helen, what happened?"

"You must have sewn one of the strips upside down."

"Can we fix it?"

"Not without ripping out half of your seams. Don't worry about it. Most people won't even notice it."

"I will," I muttered stubbornly.

"Because you know it's there. What you have is an Amish quilt. Amish women always sew one block out of place. The flaw reminds them that they're sinners and only God is perfect."

"Well, I wanted a perfect quilt."

"I know the feeling. When you've put this much work into something, you always hope for a master-piece."

Helen didn't give me a chance to mope. She helped me sandwich together the quilt top, fluffy batting, and a backing sheet and fasten the whole business in the quilt frame. "Now comes the patience part," she said. "We unroll this like a scroll and stitch around every diamond with a needle and thread."

The handwork was soothing—almost as good as stroking beneath a mattress—and after a while I got the hang of it. "You know what?" I said as I worked eight tiny stitches onto my needle and pushed it through with my thimble. "I think I'll take home ec with Alice this fall."

✦

At lunchtime, Ona Mae blew up because I said I didn't like asparagus.

"What do you mean, you don't like asparagus? Here we are supplying you with food from our table and you *don't like asparagus!*"

Laura Nell's eyes popped. Jackie and Theodore froze, their forks in mid-air.

"I'm sorry," I said.

"Didn't your mother teach you any manners?"

"Ona Mae," said Helen. "Calm down."

The boys were staring at their plates, but Laura Nell's googly eyes were darting from me to Ona Mae and back again.

"My mother taught me lots of things," I said through clenched teeth. Although I could hear Effie telling me to watch my mouth, Ona Mae had pushed me too far. "For one, people don't like looking at a sourpuss face."

"You ungrateful little brat. There are starving people out there—"

"So give them my asparagus." I threw down my napkin and ran to the only place in the house where I'd found refuge—Helen's room.

Helen followed me in and tried to smooth things over. "Don't let Ona Mae's temper get you down. She's got a lot on her mind right now. More kids, more work, more responsibilities."

"I didn't ask to be sent here."

"I know that."

"She didn't like me from the jump-go."

"She doesn't know you yet. Give her some time."

"I'll give her thirteen days and not one minute more."

"Here," Helen said, handing me some money. "Ride Laura Nell's bike to the store and buy some quilting thread. Maybe that'll cool you off."

I jumped astraddle of that bike, pedaled like crazy, and was back at the house in twenty minutes. In the hallway, when I passed the first bedroom and heard Ona Mae say "asparagus," I stopped to listen shamelessly at the door. I thought she was talking on the phone, until I heard Martin say, "Is *that* why you called me home?"

"That girl's got an attitude problem."

"It's no wonder. I told you what her home was like and—"

"She's not at her home now. She's in *our* home, and I'll not tolerate her mouthing back at me."

"Cut her some slack. You haven't exactly been Miss Mary Sunshine yourself."

"Oh, no, you don't, Martin Quincy. Don't you go laying the blame on me. You're the one who's responsible for this fine state of affairs."

"I know that, and I'm trying to make it right."

"Nothing about this is right. It wasn't right what you did fourteen years ago. It wasn't right for you to go running off like a madman when you saw that picture in the paper. For all you know, there might have been a dozen different men."

"Mary Margaret wasn't a tramp. She was a lonely girl, and I was a lonely guy, and we needed each other at the time."

"But you can't really be sure that you're the father."

"The fingers, Ona Mae. She's got my crooked little fingers."

I stared at my princess pinkies, thunderstruck, as Martin's words sank in. That overbearing, obnoxious, nit-picking man was my father. The All-American dad I'd dreamed about.

"Maybe you can feel sorry for Mary Margaret, but I can't," said Ona Mae. "The ink wasn't even dry on our marriage license when she wrote and told you she was pregnant."

I must have made a noise, because Martin jerked

the door open. When he saw me, his face went white and he said, "Freedom?"

I tore away from him and blasted out the front door. Down the ramp, down the sidewalk, down the tree-lined street.

"Freedom!" Martin called. "Come back!"

His voice only made me run faster. At the highway, I darted onto the pavement and stopped at the center line to let a tractor-trailer zoom past. It whizzed by with an angry blast of its air horn, its exhaust stinging my nostrils and making my stomach heave.

I raced on for another couple of blocks before a searing pain in my side forced me to slow down. I looked back. There was no sign of Martin.

Sweat oozed from my body, soaking my new white shirt. Tears scratched at my eyes, but I blinked them back and hurried on. I was going home where I belonged—home to Dogwood Lane.

When I reached our apartment, I tiptoed onto the front porch and tried the door quietly, so as not to alert Effie. Locked. I slipped around to the back. It was locked, too, but I found a piece of cardboard in the alley and slid it between the screen door and the jamb to knock the hook off its latch.

Walking past the deep freeze and into the kitchen, I was struck by the silence. No buzzing from the refrigerator, no ticking from the wall clock.

Miss Harbaugh must have paid the back rent and given the landlord a piece of her mind. The kitchen was newly painted, and it smelled of insecticide. The floor and counter top were littered with roach bodies, belly up, looking like flattened raisins.

I needed a drink, needed to splash cold water on my face, but when I turned on the faucet, no water came out. I went back to the porch and opened the deep freeze, hoping to find a jug of ice. The electricity had been cut off, and I almost threw up from the stench of rotten chili. I grabbed a milk jug full of water and quietly closed the lid.

At the sink, I washed my face and took a drink. The water was warm, but it didn't taste bad and it shaved the edge off my thirst.

My stomach hurt. My head ached. I wandered through the apartment, feeling and smelling the emptiness. How I missed Mama! I wanted to touch her, talk to her. I pulled back the covers on her bed, then lay down and buried my face in her pillowcase. Shampoo and whiskey. If I lived to be a hundred, I would associate that combination of smells with my mother.

I ran my hand between the mattress and box springs, and worked it farther and farther toward the center to feel the coolness of the fabric. My fingers touched something stiff—a piece of paper? I pulled it out and sat up when I saw it was an envelope with Martin's return address. This had to be the letter Mama'd hidden from me, to keep me from meddling in her "private business." I yanked it out and read the small, precise writing:

> July 5
> Mary Margaret:
> I apologize for the scene at your house last
> night, but you have to realize I was in shock

after seeing a front-page picture of my daughter.

We have to work through this problem like sensible adults. You've had Freedom for thirteen years, and it's high time I got a share of her, too. I propose that we meet somewhere on neutral ground and discuss the situation. I am, of course, willing to help you financially. If your home is any indication, you can certainly use the money.

I hope we can spare our families the pain and publicity of legal proceedings, but if you refuse my offer, I'll have no choice but to take you to court. I doubt you want that, since your drinking will surely become an issue. Please give my proposal serious consideration and then call me at 555-3357 (during office hours).

Martin

I read the letter again and felt a blinding fury. Wanting his share. Offering Mama money. Call him during office hours. What was this—a business proposition? With me as the commodity?

I wadded up the letter and fired it across the room. Martin Quincy might be my biological father, but he most certainly was not my dad. He hadn't walked the floor with me or changed my diapers or paid my doctor bills. He was a cold, heartless, calculating man. No wonder Mama had kept his identity a secret.

Mama. My hand flew to my mouth. What a shock

it must have been for her to receive my letter, telling her I was living with Martin and Ona Mae. I fell back across her bed and cried. The pain no longer centered on my stomach. It was a horrible, crushing ache in my soul.

✦

A ringing sound awoke me. The room was dark except for a shaft of light at the window. Where was I? Then I remembered. Mama's room. And that must be Effie's telephone ringing.

I felt my way down the dark hall and into the kitchen, so I could listen through the wall.

". . . haven't seen the child," said Effie. "I told you I'd call if she shows up here."

Poor Effie. I knew she was worried about me, but I wasn't ready to be found just yet. I went back to Mama's room, stretched out on her bed, and let my thoughts run wild.

Martin had caught Mama off guard on the Fourth and found her drunk. He'd seen our apartment at its worst—smelly garbage, dirty dishes, turtle tinkle on the floor. He'd put Mama to the test, and she'd failed, miserably. Now he was planning to take me away from her. Buy me.

How much was I worth to him? Five hundred dollars? A thousand? Two thousand?

The thought of him as my father made me sick. Mama's troubles the past thirteen years could be laid at Martin's feet. He'd taken advantage of her that graduation summer when she was scared and vulnerable. Before Farmer Boy left Gabriel, he'd sowed that one last crop—me.

The bump on my nose, the crooked fingers. Both were flaws that came from Martin. I pictured Theodore, all angles and elbows and gonky like me. My half brother. He, too, had gotten the worst from Martin's genetic pool.

But Theodore had auburn hair. An ugly, croaky sound escaped my throat when I thought about Ona Mae. No wonder she didn't like me. I was an illegitimate child, a reminder that her precious Marty Q had been with another woman before her.

Hours later, I was still awake. And cold. I curled up into a ball and tried to draw warmth into myself.

✦

I awoke and glanced at Mama's watch. Ten o'clock. The room was hot and stuffy, and a golden beam of sunlight was cooking me on the bed. As I changed position, dust motes swirled and dipped in the beam, crazily, like my thoughts.

I pictured Mama lying here the day after my birthday, unconscious from the booze and sleeping pills. Other memories rose up to haunt me. I saw her buttering day-old treats from the bakery. I saw her polishing my spelling trophy. I heard her declaration that I'd be Somebody Someday.

I, Freedom Avery, was a smart girl, a big-shot whiz kid. But somewhere along the way, I'd failed to recognize the big, important truths in life: Love is day-old cinnamon rolls when you can't afford fresh. Love is wanting something better for your child than you've ever had yourself. Love is drying out at a treatment center, so you won't lose your only daughter.

"I love you, Mama," I said out loud. I dragged myself off the bed and went to use the bathroom. Out of habit, I flushed the stool. It responded with a loud gurgle as it emptied the last of the water in the tank, and I knew that Effie would have heard it and guessed that I was here.

I didn't mind now, giving away my hiding place. I needed a hug, something to eat, and Effie's shoulder to lean on.

Effie gave me the hug, fixed me some bacon and eggs, and sat down to put her teeth in. "Martin came here last night looking for you, and Ona Mae called early this morning."

When I didn't answer, she said, "Freedom, I thought you were a fighter, and I'm surprised at you, running away from your troubles. First you ran away from Miss Harbaugh, and now from your own father."

I stopped chewing. "I thought you didn't know who my father was."

"I didn't, until Mary Margaret told me yesterday."

"You talked to Mama?"

"She called here, mad as hops. Before that, she called the Child Protection Agency, to find out how they could put you kids in the Quincys' home. They haven't lived here long enough to be approved as foster parents by the state."

"And?"

"Miss Harbaugh told her that when Martin saw on the news where you kids had disappeared, he called the police. They referred him to her, and she gave him the whole story. When he said he wanted temporary custody, she told him to get proof that he was your father."

"And he did?"

"Drove straight to Jefferson City and got a copy of your birth certificate, and sure enough, his name was on it. They had an emergency hearing, and the judge granted him temporary custody and asked if he'd be willing to take Jackie, too. Said he'd be better off with you at the Quincys' than in a foster home in another county."

"Martin's had people bowing and scraping to him all down the line. It's not fair. He caused the trouble in the first place, by sowing his wild oats fourteen years ago."

"It takes two to get that job done, child. Don't forget your mother was in on it, too."

"Effie, how is Mama? Other than being mad, I mean."

"OK, I guess, but that treatment she's going through sounds like torture to me."

I twiddled my fork. I knew about torture. Torture was being thirteen years old and finding out the Inspector General is your father.

"She gets two shots first thing every morning—one to close the little flap leading to her stomach, and the other to make her nauseated. Then they take her to a room that's fixed up like a bar—dark, with honky-tonk music—and give her some liquor to drink."

"Liquor? But—"

"One of the shots keeps the alcohol from getting to her stomach, and the other makes her throw it right back up."

"Oh, yuk." I looked away from the puddle of egg yolk on my plate.

"After that, they make her stay in bed for several hours without washing her face or brushing her teeth, and she has to keep smelling a cloth that's been dipped in alcohol. She suffers the effects of a hangover while she's totally sober. Eventually, just the smell of liquor will make her sick."

I groaned. Mama was doing that for me.

"What's the matter now?"

"In my letter, I said she was on vacation."

"I doubt it's as good as Hawaii."

As usual, Effie helped me get a handle on things. She listened as I poured my heart out and told her all that was wrong with the Quincys. When I finished, she said, "Freedom, temporary custody is just that—temporary. As soon as Mary Margaret gets home, you'll be moving back here." She paused to wipe her face with her apron and give me a clackety grin. "It seems to me that any girl who can fend for herself in the wilderness for a week can surely stand a few more days with a nit-picker and a sourpuss."

I hugged her tight and kissed her withered cheek. "You win. I won't like it, but I'll go back. Freedom Jo Avery's not a quitter."

"Child, I never doubted you for a minute."

26
THE SLUGGER

Fifteen minutes later, I was at the Quincys'. Seeing Martin's car in the driveway, I drew a deep breath, preparing for the showdown.

Martin and Ona Mae came into the living room when they heard the front door open. He hadn't shaved, and his shirt was wrinkled. She wasn't wearing makeup. I lasered in on his fingers. Both pinkies were shaped like a "C."

"Freedom. Thank goodness," he said. "We've searched all over town. Where've you been, anyway?"

"Home. *My* home."

Martin winced. "I understand your anger at being deceived. Please, can't we sit down and talk?" He drew Ona Mae to the couch. I sat gingerly on a chair and scuffed my toe along a seam in the hardwood floor.

"This whole situation came as a shock to us, too," Martin said. "We moved back here, not knowing Mary Margaret was in Gabriel, not knowing about you."

I glared at him. How I wanted to wipe that self-righteous expression off his face. "And now you're trying to take me away from Mama. It won't work. I love my mother. I don't even like you."

"There goes the mouth again," sighed Ona Mae.

Ignoring her, I took another shot at Martin. "Why didn't you just tell me the truth from the start?"

"I wanted you to get to know me first. I was afraid Mary Margaret had poisoned your mind against me."

I dug my nails into the arms of the chair, and imagined him dangling money in front of Mama like a carrot in front of a mule. "You can't buy me, you know. I'm not for sale."

"What? What are you talking about?"

"I found the letter you sent Mama. Offering her money. Making a proposal. The perfect businessman, cutting a deal."

"I was offering to pay child support, in exchange for visiting rights."

"Then why tell her to call during business hours?"

"So she and Ona Mae wouldn't have to talk to each other."

He had it all worked out. Logical, sensible, cold as ice. The Inspector General at his best.

"I didn't want to make things harder for Ona Mae than they already are," Martin went on. "She suffered through this, too. We were newlyweds in Germany when Mary Margaret wrote and told me she was pregnant. Just imagine how that news would affect a new bride." He laid his hand on Ona Mae's and looked into her eyes.

Was that the way he'd looked at Mama? Had she been putty in his hands?

"Ona Mae got a job at the army base, and we sent

Mary Margaret a check every two weeks until you were born.''

"Why stop then?" I spouted. "Babies have to eat, you know."

"Because your mother lied to—"

I clamped my hands over my ears. "Don't say it. I won't listen to one blamed word against my mother."

"OK, OK," Martin said, so I took my hands down. "Just let me say I'm sorry for the way I've handled this. I was working new ground here, and I made some mistakes. But can't we start over? I want to be a father to you."

I gave him my iciest stare. "No!" He drew back as if I'd slapped him, but I plowed ahead, wanting to hurt him for hurting Mama. "Once the new wears off, you'll start picking me apart. I've seen how you treat Theodore. Ridiculing him, criticizing him. The very same thing your dad did to you."

His face registered shock, and I felt a grim satisfaction.

"Martin," said Ona Mae in a small voice, "you do expect Theodore to do and be all the things you couldn't."

"That's not so."

"Yes, it is. I—I guess I noticed it more when you started fawning over Freedom."

"Fawning? I was just trying to make her feel welcome, wanted. You certainly weren't." Martin ran a hand over his eyes. "Oh, what's the use? My daughter's a little spitfire who wants nothing to do with me, and my wife accuses me of *fawning*. I give up." He snatched his keys off the table and stalked out of the house.

"Don't, Marty," cried Ona Mae as she ran after him.

I watched out the window, uncertain, when he waved her away and drove off. Ona Mae had sided with me over Theodore. Now that was a switch. Not wanting to face her, I headed upstairs.

In the shower, I tried to wash away my confusion. I should feel justified at hurting Martin, but I felt guilty instead. A little voice—my conscience, maybe—told me I should have heard Martin out. Mama had lied about *what*?

As I left the bathroom, the sound of laughter drew me to Theodore's room, where he and Jackie were bent over a project at the desk. It made me choke up inside, seeing my two brothers together and knowing I was the link that connected them. What would happen after this "temporary arrangement" came to an end? I had an extra brother now, and an aunt, who was also my friend. If I refused to let Martin be a father to me, I'd have to stop seeing them.

I moseyed into the room. The boys were working on a black, bat-shaped model plane. "B-2 Stealth Bomber," I read from the box. "Isn't that the new Air Force plane?"

"Yep," said Theodore. "Two billion dollars' worth. It flies so fast and low, it evades radar."

Evades? There was nothing wrong with this kid's brain. All he needed was for Martin to ease off. I studied him for a minute. He'd be cute someday, when he outgrew the gonkiness. Touching his bony shoulder, I said, "I guess you guys know about Martin and me."

"Dad told us last night. You're my sister."

"Just somebody else to boss you around," said Jackie.

I resisted the urge to hug both of them, and left the room. As I was going downstairs, I met Ona Mae coming up, carrying some blue satin fabric and glittery trim. "Is that the robe for King Herod?"

She stared at me for a long time before answering. Her eyes were red, and she still wasn't wearing makeup. "Yes, if I ever get it made. I haven't sewed a stitch in years."

"I could help. I like to sew."

The words surprised me almost as much as they did Ona Mae. "You'd do that?" she said.

"I've never used a pattern, but I could get Helen to show me how."

"I'll show you. I remember that much. Time's running out. Want to start this afternoon?"

I nodded, then went on downstairs, feeling as if I'd crashed over Niagara Falls in a rowboat and come out alive.

27

MENDING

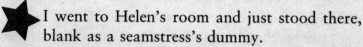 I went to Helen's room and just stood there, blank as a seamstress's dummy.

She looked up from working on my quilt and smiled. "It's about time you got back. You must have gone to China for that thread."

"Sorry," I mumbled.

"Don't worry about it. I wasn't completely out. Grab a needle and thread, and let's see if we can mend the fabric of your life, or at least get a few more stitches in this quilt."

"I think the fabric of my life came from somebody's ragbag," I said as I picked up my thimble and sat down.

"I'm sorry you had to find out about Martin by accident. I thought from the beginning it was a mistake to keep the secret."

"I'm used to secrets. Mama kept him a secret my whole life."

"I'm sure she was devastated when he married Ona Mae. They had quite a romance going for a while."

"I've got to say this, even if he is your brother. I can't figure out what Mama saw in him."

"It all started the night of the fire. He came to my house and got her something to wear besides a party dress, and he spent the next few days just being with her. Later on, he helped her find a job and a place to live. Ona Mae got so jealous, she broke up with him. They were all so young. I think Martin mistook Mary Margaret's dependency for love."

"But why would Mama choose him to lean on? Other friends were there that night. Dorothy told me so."

"His chivalry, I guess. You see, Martin got so mad at a reporter bugging Mary Margaret, he slugged him. Broke his nose."

"Martin?" I squeaked. "I thought it was Lanny B!"

"Lanny B was all talk and no action."

I stood up, shoving the thimble into my pocket. "It's hot in here. I've got to get some air."

I went outside and started pacing on sun-baked sidewalks. My head was spinning from the people and events flashing through my mind. Mama dancing at a party. Martin pointing a rifle at his father. Theodore crying over a ball game. Mama screaming at a fire. Martin punching a reporter. A knight brandishing a sword.

My feet carried me to the gates of the cemetery, where pink and red flowers sprouted from concrete urns. To escape the whizzing traffic on the outer road, I entered the gates and stood gazing at the gently rolling lawn.

For some reason, I felt drawn to Mama's family, and I headed toward the angel statue near the Avery monument. As I walked, my tennis shoes whispered secrets to the grass.

At a stone marked "Quincy," I stopped to read the names and dates. Laura Lee and Howard Martin Quincy. They had to be my other set of grandparents. In my mind, I saw a Jewelry Box quilt, an heirloom, a treasure on a trunk. I saw a pair of overalls, faded, holes in the knees, hanging on a nail.

When I neared the graves of Mama's folks, I sat on a concrete bench under a shade tree. At last, I felt alone enough to think—about me and who I was, exactly.

Freedom Jo Avery.

A gonky girl with a hump on her nose and crooked fingers. A girl who was slowly but surely gaining an understanding of her mother. A girl who had told her father, in no uncertain terms, that she wanted no part of him. A girl who would always have a hole in her soul.

A pigeon landed on the angel statue to preen and peck. I watched it until it flew away, and then I read the names on the monument. Charles and Marie, my grandparents, lying between Thomas Jackson and Josie Ann.

Jackie had been named after Mama's brother. The "Jo" in my name had been for Josie Ann. Our names had been a way for Mama to connect the broken threads of her family. To mend the fabric of her life.

Maybe Martin kept his father's overalls, not to punish himself, but to mend the fabric of *his* life.

Wiping my sweaty hands on my shorts, I noticed a

tiny lump in my pocket. The thimble. I placed it on my finger and idly scraped it on the bench.

My mind drifted to the Freedom quilt. I'd put it together one strip at a time, each segment building on the last. Only when I'd stood back and viewed the quilt as a whole had I noticed the two diamonds out of place. Each strip had seemed so insignificant—until it was connected to the others.

Could that principle apply to people, too? Martin had been scarred by an alcoholic father. Mama, by the loss of her family. Fourteen years ago, when they needed each other, they'd created me. Like each strip in my quilt, I was affected by what had gone before.

I thought of Amish women, misplacing blocks in their quilts, to remind them that no one except God is perfect. Both of my parents had flaws, and their parents before them. I had a few flaws myself. Smart-mouthed. Bullheaded.

I hadn't given up on my Freedom quilt, and I wouldn't give up on Martin. I just hoped he hadn't given up on me. A hot tear rolled down my cheek, and I brushed it away with my hand. Suddenly, I knew I had to find him—to start over, make peace. I wanted something more from my father than a pair of over-alls. I jumped up and took off running.

A car was parked between me and the gates. Martin's car. Had he followed me here? No, there he was—kneeling at his father's grave, crying. I inched over to a tombstone, as if the shiny granite would shield me from his pain. The thimble on my finger clinked against the stone.

Martin stumbled to his feet, his eyes wide with

surprise. "Freedom? I—I— What are you doing here?" he said as the sunlight glinted off his rings.

"The same as you, I guess—thinking things through."

"Did it help?"

"Yes. Yes, it did." His eyes locked with mine. I saw past the inspector into the soul of a little boy who'd wet the bed, and I read his yearning for acceptance.

He must have looked beyond the spitfire in me and seen the hole in my soul. "Freedom," he said, "we've got a lot to learn about each other. I want us to have that chance. With my dad, I carried a grudge for too long, and didn't get to know the real person inside. I don't want that to happen with you and me."

"Neither do I."

"From here on out, I'm going to be the perfect father to you and Theodore. You set me straight this morning. I've been beating him down, I guess because of the way my dad did me. Which brings me around to your mother. Mary Margaret's had her problems, but she's done a good job with you. You're strong and smart and self-sufficient."

"And smart-mouthed and bullheaded."

"That, too," said Martin, grinning. He withdrew a folded slip of paper from his pocket and handed it to me. "That's why I dug this out to show you exactly why I've been an absentee father all these years."

I unfolded the paper, and Mama's handwriting seemed to jump off the page: "My little girl was born dead this morning. Now you've got your freedom, and I've got mine. Mary Margaret."

I was stunned. My name wasn't patriotic after all.

It was Mama's way of asserting her independence, of bowing out of Martin's and Ona Mae's lives. At nineteen years old, she'd been willing to raise me by herself. It was absolute, undeniable proof that she cherished me. "May I keep this?" I murmured, clutching the note to my chest.

"If you like." Martin held out a hand to me. "What say we go home now?"

I stared at his hand, at the crooked little finger. It was now or never to tell him how I felt, or he'd always come across as the inspector. "I have to level with you first. You're too particular, too neat, too perfect. It drives me crazy that you keep turning the 'Coo' on the cookie jar. I don't want a perfect father. I'd prefer an ordinary dad."

"*You're* the one moving the cookie jar? I thought it was Laura Nell." Martin threw back his head and laughed, and the sound was like rolling thunder in that silent place.

I started laughing, too. How fitting that Laura Nell had been blamed for the *cookies*. We'd evened the score. I caught Martin's hand and went with him to the car. As we drove away, I looked back toward my ancestors' graves. I wished I could have known them. It was as though their living, and even their dying, had created what was me.

"Mighty healthy flowers for July," said Martin, pointing at the flowers in their urns.

"Geraniums." They reminded me of Effie's pots on the porch, brightening their little corner of the world. I reread Mama's note, then moved the thimble to my crooked little finger. My mother, my father—they both loved me. Mary Margaret and Marty Q. I giggled. From here on out, they'd both have a share of Freedom.